Perfect Pleasures
An Anthology Of Romantic Erotica

Cameron Lincoln

Copyright © 2013 Cameron Lincoln

Cover images © Artem Furman – Fotolia.com

Cover design by Cameron Lincoln

All rights reserved.

ISBN-13: 978-1505929669

ISBN-10: 1505929660

DEDICATION

For my lady.

Your unwavering support and love is appreciated, adored and forever returned.

CONTENTS

	Acknowledgments	i
1	Defined – *A Poem*	1
2	Maria Unchained	2
3	Vanilla – *A Poem*	20
4	Focus	22
5	The Madison Banquet	44
6	Power – *A Poem*	64
7	Submissive Desire	65
8	Closing Time At Pulse	105
9	Nylon – *A Poem*	110
10	Mile High Nylons	111
11	Dressed – *A Poem*	121
12	A Friendly Rivalry	122
13	Landscape – *A Poem*	149
14	Extra Marital Pleasures	150
15	Painted – *A Poem*	178

ACKNOWLEDGMENTS

Thank you to Lisa Fulham, Paige Thomas, Chris Kuhn and Amanda Carrington, for their friendship and unwavering belief in me. I don't know what I did to deserve such good friends.

Thanks to each and every one of my supporters and friends on the world wide web. Every one of your kind words, bursts of encouragement and support made this possible. I couldn't have dreamed of this book existing without you. I could fill a whole other tome listing people, but I hope dearly that you all know you are, and how important you've been on this journey.

Thanks to you, whoever you are, wherever you may be, for reading this book. I hope it gives you even a fraction of the pleasure I had in writing it.

DEFINED
A Poem

Scrambling for meaning,
To etch in words
A moment, a feeling.
To fix it in time.

But we flux and we shift,
And we're never the same
From now until then,
Up to what we'll become.

Each encounter brings change,
Perceptions cascade.
It's all what you make it,
So make it your own.

All that's determined is
Nothing means more,
Than the journey you take
To arrive in these arms.

MARIA UNCHAINED

1

Maria was lost.

Not in terms of geography, because she had memorized the address and knew herself to be mere moments away from her destination.

She was lost within the world, struggling against its pressures, a victim of circumstance and regret. It was those things that had brought her here today. She did not want to continue at this pace knowing that she had lost herself, changed by the years into someone she often did not recognise in the mirror.

Maria was as nervous as she had ever been. She was starting to think that the whole thing had been a mistake, a foolish choice made while angry at things she couldn't control.

She walked deeper into the wide alleyway as the midday sun beat down. The noise of the traffic passing was distant, muffled, and she took careful, tentative steps down this access road to the warehouse district. Huge, anonymous buildings loomed on each side, dwarfing her.

No, she did *not* regret her decision today. She was second guessing herself. This choice had been made carefully, meticulously. Now that she was moments away from going through with it, it filled her with an anxiety. A fun, enjoyable, perverse anxiety. What would it be like? How would it feel? Would she be the same afterwards, or changed in some way, fundamentally altered at a cellular level, rewired to appreciate the act of physical love in an entirely different way? She hoped so.

There were access doors leading to the various storage facilities, work areas, and small offices housed within these buildings; non descript, plain doors behind which a myriad of jobs were going on. All manner of potential secrets.

A door up ahead swung open and released someone into the sunlight: a blonde woman in jeans and a T-shirt with a bag slung at her hip. She was sauntering, carefree, her mind elsewhere. Her cheeks were flushed, healthy and vibrant; whatever she had been up to in the place towards which Maria now walked, she had left lighter than air. She passed Maria with a knowing, placid smile, like she knew where Maria was headed.

The door clicked shut. It was a door that held the best kept secret in town, the kind known by only a few and passed on to others only with careful consideration. She slowed, relishing this build up, the sense of impending excitement.

When finally she reached it she took a breath.

This was it.

She pushed the buzzer by the speaker set into the doorframe. A tinny voice emerged from the grille: "Hello, Cherry Blossom Global."

"The weather is awfully lovely today, isn't it?" she said carefully, enunciating every word the way she had been instructed to. There was a pause, then the speaker buzzed and she heard the door unlatch.

Here we go, she thought, and pushed her way inside.

2

Maria sank half of her glass of wine in one pull and had to refrain from downing the whole thing. Across the table, Sally made a look of wide-eyed surprise.

"Take it easy, tigress," she laughed.

"It's been one of those days," Maria said, rubbing her neck and tugging idly at the collar of her blouse. "It's been one of those *years.*"

It has been one of those lives, she told herself quietly.

"I'm supposed to be the overly dramatic one," Sally said, sipping her own wine. "You're looking fantastic, anyway."

Maria knew when she was being flattered, but took the compliment. She was slim, with perfectly proportioned hips and breasts for her size, with elfin features and chestnut brown hair down to her shoulders; the style was still looking admittedly rather nice from a salon appointment two days ago. She was attractive, she knew that; enough men had approached her in bars and showed an interest for her to know that, but she was amidst an ongoing phase where she rarely felt *sexy*, truly desired. Although she adored her increasingly fleeting catch ups with her old college roommate, they always served as a reminder as to how far removed she was from her friend.

Sally, all six slender feet of her, shifted in her seat to point her tapering, perfectly toned legs out of the booth to draw the attention of any of the hotel bar's gentleman patrons, entering or exiting, or merely looking her way, as they so often did. Men loved her, but then what was not to love about a statuesque blonde, particularly one with a love of flirting and a deeper love of being a bad girl? The business suit, the hair, her whole attitude was designed to make men swoon and it took very little effort for Sally to claim one for her own fun, for as long as she would allow him to hang on.

"Thank you," Maria smiled. "I'm sure I don't need to tell you how great you're looking."

"No, but I like to hear it," she giggled.

Their friendship had endured since college, where they had started as roommates thrown together by circumstance. Though their personalities were opposites they found friendship through proximity and dependence; they had grown on each other, and got from the other what neither had. Sally brought Maria adventure and wild nights (and there *had* been some *very* wild ones, though the Maria who had taken part in them now felt like a stranger); Maria gave Sally a stable anchor, a role model for when, on that rare occasion she realised she had gone too far, she needed to ground herself and come back to Earth.

"So how is everything?" Sally asked, as if 'everything' could be summed up in one sentence. Maria thought about pouring it all out, but she was already exhausted from her day at work.

"The usual," she said. "Work's going well. Same old, same old."

"And how are those marvellous boys of yours?" Sally asked.

"Oh, they keep me busy," Maria nodded with a wry smile. Sally was not a children person, never had been and Maria doubted she ever would be; they would get in the way of her social life, of her career, of her parties and her endless fucking of strangers. Maria always kept talk of her two young sons to a minimum with Sally; her friend made all the right faces and noises and asked questions, but deep down Maria knew Sally wasn't really that interested.

"You gotta thank the asshole who gave you those two," Sally said. "Obviously he's a prick and if I see him I'll rip his heart out for fucking you over and putting it in the wind, but you can't begrudge those two."

Of course she couldn't. They were her life. They filled her with joy every time she even pictured their faces. She would give up everything for them, *had* given up so much to raise them right, to make them happy, to ensure they did not become carbon copies of their absent father.

"They just take every little piece of my energy and I don't feel like I have any time for myself," she blurted out, the wine having apparently gone straight to her head. "Some days it feels like I've forgotten who I am."

"We need to go out and find you a man," Sally explained, somewhat patronisingly.

"I don't need a man," Maria countered, swilling the last of her wine. "I need a dick that doesn't require batteries."

Sally pretended to be shocked, but it was an act. Both girls knew each other's sexual pasts, and though Maria *was* quieter, *was* the shyest of the two, she had had her moments during her youth; moments that now were such a distant memories. Both recalled late nights, sitting up drinking, explaining their darkest fantasies. In that department, Maria's had always been the most extreme…

A handsome waiter arrived to ask them if they required anything else. Sally flirted with him, laughed at his lame jokes, and he retreated without so much as a look at Maria; she was an eclipsed planet in the shade of a shining star.

When the waiter had gone, Sally caught Maria looking into her glass. She eyed her friend up for a while, then reached into her bag and produced a pen. "Girl, I'm going to do you a favour."

"What's that?" Maria asked, taking their shared bottle and refilling her glass. Another wouldn't hurt. It might make the relentless onslaught of the boys' energy a little more tolerable when she got home.

"Ring this number," Sally insisted, scribbling it down on a napkin. "I haven't tried this place yet but a lot of my girlfriends vouch for it."

"What is it?"

With a playful smile on her lips and a wicked glint in her eyes, Sally told her.

3

Maria stepped from the access road to find herself in a small anteroom lit by elegant, ornate standing lamps. The carpet beneath her feet was expensive, luxuriant, and the whole décor of the place was both regal yet welcoming. Soft, wordless music played, completely locking out the sounds of the outside world, and the place smelled of pleasing scented candles. She looked at herself in a mirror with a fine gilded frame, righting an errant strand of hair, ensuring she was presentable. It didn't matter so much — there was time for improvement, and it was only mere moments away.

A second inner door opened, revealing a woman Maria assumed to be a receptionist, though not dressed as a standard administrative assistant would be. She was stunning, tall, with almost bone-white skin, wearing a red gown which was split at the hip to reveal her wholly toned legs, perfectly pedicured toes visible in burgundy heels. A smile sat on her lips.

"Madame Maria, I presume," the lady said with an accent that would place her somewhere from Eastern Europe, though Maria could not guess where. "I am Veronique."

"Hello," she said, and shook the woman's hand, feeling like she was on a job interview.

"Everything has been taken care of. If you'd like to follow me."

She did so, pursuing the red temptress through the door and down a corridor, past sturdy wooden entrances that hid untold delights. What could possibly be going on in those chambers?

In her head played her conversation with Sally as they shared their wine.

"They cater for any fantasy," Sally had explained. "They only take women clients and they follow your instructions to the letter. No matter what you want to do. You want to be in charge? It's yours. You want to be dominated? They'll ruin you in all the ways you want."

"No way," Maria had said.

"I've only heard good reviews. Incredible reviews. Going-again-tomorrow-reviews. Worth every penny, so they say. They don't skimp on a thing. What have you go to lose?"

Maria had left their meet and picked up her boys from school, taken them home, cooked for them, played with them, exhausted them enough that finally they had surrendered to sleep; despite her endless love for them, this was often her favourite part of the day, watching them being unable to run, jump, scream and fight.

She ran herself a bath and sank into its soothing depths, holding the napkin on which Sally had written, staring at the number, wondering what to do. Though Sally had led her astray in their youth, it had always been the right kind of astray.

And she hadn't done anything wild for so long! It had been months since her last sexual encounter...and she hated herself for thinking of it in those terms. A sexual encounter. Not a fuck. A sticky fumble with a guy from work, over in ten minutes, the kind of pedestrian, soon-forgotten affair that exemplified what she had come to expect in life. What, sadly, she often felt she deserved.

Her ire was rising, blood threatening to heat to the temperature of the water in which she lay.

She reached for her cell phone and dialled the number with steady hands. The woman she spoke to had been understanding and completely discreet, laying out the service and waiting patiently for Maria to describe what she wanted. The words and scenarios that came out of Maria's mouth were in her voice, but spoken by another version of herself, younger and freer and desperate to try all the things she knew one day she would be too buttoned up or tied down to try.

She hung up, dried herself off, and fell into a restful, undisturbed sleep.

Now she was here. The anticipation of two days wait had built and every fibre of her thrummed with the notion of what she was about to do.

The assistant led her to a thick wooden door and gestured to the handle.

"Have fun, Madame," she said, and slunk away with catlike grace. Maria watched her go until she was alone in the corridor, listening to her own nervous silence.

It was now or never, and never was such an ugly thought.

She turned the handle and slipped inside.

It was a dressing room, decked out to look like backstage at a 1950s burlesque show: a vanity mirror surrounded by light bulbs; folding changing screens; mannequin torsos modeling clothes. But they were not just any clothes. Everything shone in the light, shiny and reflective; leather and rubber; PVC in a variety of colours; bustiers, corsets, boots and gloves. It was a fetishists paradise.

Amidst the sheen of vinyl, she saw it immediately and knew it was the one, sculpted so close to the mannequin it seemed to be woven into it. It was her size, perfectly.

Wait, she thought. *Enjoy this.*

There was wine waiting for her by the mirror, a crisp sauvignon blanc chilled to perfection. She sipped a glass as she surveyed the selection of fresh Yves Saint Laurent makeup that had been laid out for her. She rarely wore much, and certainly never anything so expensive and elegant, but today was special. She wore a shade of dark red lipstick, applying it carefully, loving how it left a perfect imprint of her lip on the rim of her wine glass when she drank. She tenderly applied eyeliner and mascara, ensuring it was thick enough that it would run when it was made to.

She undressed slowly, watching herself do it with a voyeur's eyes, savouring the whole experience, shedding the costume of her everyday life to reveal the truth of the woman underneath: beautiful, natural, desperate to be caressed and played with.

Desperate to be used.

First she put on the stockings, stretching them across her toes and calves, loving the sensation; wearing stockings was one of the few pleasures of dressing for work. The black seam traced a perfect line up the back of her shapely legs, and the ornate and decorative band clung to her thighs. Then came the boots, vinyl, sliding over her legs and to her knees, creaking with satisfying stiffness with every step. She paraded around, imagining herself preparing to go on stage, to be leered at, to be worshipped.

She put on the wet look sleeves that went from wrist to elbow, with a small nylon hook that went over the middle finger on each hand.

Then came the corset. With an intake of breath she slid it on and it sealed itself to her like a skin, an exterior coating of thick liquid, holding that breath in her lungs, the first reminder, a *constant* reminder of both what she wanted and why she was here. It was cut below her breasts, not digging into them but pressing, ever present, and raising them to look more wonderful than she had ever seen them. She reached back and managed to zip it up. Its lower rim hugged her hips and tapered at the front in a V that mirrored her own bare sex, which she had tended to this morning with a bath time groom, sculpting a tufted runway to her sacred entrance.

Now she went to the mirror again and looked.

She was herself, but not; some would have said this was an act, a pretence, but they could not be more wrong. This was *her*. The Maria of youth, of wild abandon, before life had put its covenants upon her. This was the caged lioness, about to be unleashed back into the wild.

She closed her eyes and inhaled as deeply as the constrictive corset would allow, taking her last snatch of air before diving beneath the surface. She said the words aloud that she had told them she would, the trigger to her fantasy.

"Come and get me."

The room fell to darkness. The frame of light bulbs left a ghostly afterimage then faded into oblivion. In the pitch black, the only sound was that of her shallow, expectant breathing. She stayed that way for several interminable seconds.

Maria was listening for footsteps but none came. She thought she heard someone else in the room, but when she listened closer there was no such sound.

And then there were strong hands upon her, reaching from behind, one going to her throat and clasping it tightly, the other to her wrist, twisting it into place in the small of her back. A hard body pushed itself against her back and a booted foot kicked her feet apart. She let out a mewling whimper, uncontrollable.

A cheek pushed against hers, clean shaven, and she smelled aftershave in the blackness. A mouth, so close to her ear she felt his hot breath, said in an earth trembling baritone: "What do we have here?"

"A slave," she whispered, barely more than a whisper. "Your slave."

The strong hands relaxed then returned to her throat. She felt a band of cold leather against the skin there, wrapping around and tightening, making each breath catch on its way to her lungs. The collar closed. She felt the slender chain that was attached go taut and she followed the mystery man where he led, through the black, careful with every step. He led her through the room and she felt the atmosphere change as they passed through an unseen doorway; they were in a wider space now, her footsteps echoing on cold stone.

She went fifteen feet or so, then her guide said: "Kneel."

"I can't see," she explained quietly.

Those hands were on her bare shoulders now, forcing her down with tremendous pressure. Her knees buckled and hit the concrete, protectively padded in her boots but she thrilled at the feeling of discomfort that shot through her. The chain went taut again as she heard him moving around.

A match sparked in the darkness and went to a candle mounted on an iron stand, then another a few inches away, then another. He went to several more of these, lighting them slowly, deliberately, each new flame revealing more of the surroundings. Her eyes adjusted to the candle light and she saw she was kneeling in the centre of a half dozen of these candelabras.

She was the centre of attention.

Immediately behind her was a construct of reflective steel and padded leather cushions, the sort of device that could hold a body in various positions: lying down, kneeling, trussed up. There were leather straps across it, long enough to secure ankles and wrists…

In front of her was a chair. High backed and padded. His chair.

His *throne*.

The light did not extend far beyond the circle, but she could see cold steel rafters glinting above. This was a warehouse, converted for her purposes. That this much space was devoted entirely to her was a delight.

The candle light illuminated *him* too, a god in a finely pressed business suit. He was almost sculpted, with an impossibly tight chest shoulders so broad she imagined him struggling to pass through doorways, and arms on which, despite his perfectly tailored garments, she swore she could see every taut muscle. He was pristinely handsome, a strong jaw, his hair slicked back and combed to perfection, traces of grey at the temples. He was a confident man with experience and poise. Her guide. Her Master.

He completed his circle, lighting the last candle, retreated into the gloom and returned, sitting on his throne and coiling her chain around his powerful fist, pulling her closer, making her crawl, subservient.

His dark eyes bored into hers so fiercely she thought she would combust. He thrust a foot closer to her and her hands went to it, feeling steel-hard calf muscles beneath his expensive garb. They worked up, across his thighs, approaching the outline of his hidden phallus, an impressive bulge within his clothes.

As her fingers almost touched it, a stinging slap whipped across her face and she recoiled only as far as her leash would allow.

"You don't get that gift yet."

From the darkness beneath the chair he produced a toy; a thick rod of rubber seven inches long, fitted at the base with a stretching band of fabric. He fastened it around his thigh, the toy pointing skyward, inches from his real but hidden rod.

"Sit," he demanded.

Maria placed her legs on either side of his thigh and he guided her down without hesitation; the thick rubber length kissed her lower abdomen then found its target, parting lips that had been moist and ready ever since the lights had gone off in the dressing room. She cried out and it echoed all around the empty warehouse.

With her leash coiled around his forearm, Master's hand went to the fleshy white meat of her buttocks and squeezed tightly, fingers drifting down to tickle her spread lips as she rode the dildo he wore. His other hand cupped and squeezed her breasts in turn, pinching and twisting her nipples just enough to bring satisfying barbs of pain. All the while he watched her, stared into and *through* her, eye contact she couldn't break.

Her chest flushed robin-red in no time, the passion building, the glory of the sensations in her welcoming box spilling through her, alerting her body to every breeze, every drop of sweat that beaded on her dove white skin.

Maria rolled towards her orgasm, hips grinding against him. "Choke me," she begged. "Slap me." He did so, one vice like grip on her throat, starving her of oxygen to bring spots to her vision. His thick fingers shuddered the flesh on her cheek with every quick blow.

Her first climax tore through her and her screaming rang through the open space like a thousand ricocheting bullets. With strength so rich it barely felt like an effort he immediately forced her upwards by the throat, off the dildo, and a small but gushing fount of misty liquid spilled from her quivering sex, staining his pants on the thigh and crotch.

"I'm sorry," she said weakly, trying to get her footing, but her legs were shaking so hard and her heels were so precarious that she slumped backwards.

Master was there to catch her, protective, powerful, but he was angry now, and within a second she found herself lying with her back against the steel and leather bench facing his throne. He plucked the strap-on from his dense thigh and fastened her in to the bench as her orgasm faded; she was bent backwards over the thing, her arms and legs flush with the supports of it, bound quickly in place with studded belt straps. Her head rested on a small, hard padded cushion. Her pearl-like tits pointed at the ceiling. She was helpless.

"You ruined my suit," he said, and she quietly thrilled at what had happened; she had squirted once before during a late night drunken tumble in her youth, and had never been able to repeat it. Now she was happy that it added another layer to her scenario.

"Sorry, sir," Maria said. "Punish me. Please."

Her mouth didn't have time to close; the dildo she had just ridden was forced inside, over extending her jaw and plunging into the hot depths of her throat. She gagged instantly, bringing up a wave of saliva that coated the rubber baton and frothed at her red lips. He worked it like a blunt dagger into her mouth, back and forth, each thrust making her choke.

Give me it, she thought. *I'll take anything you throw at me, swallow it with a smile.*

As Maria chugged the length, tasting herself on the tart rubber, she heard the high pitched whine of a vibrator, and through tear-speckled eyes she saw him brandishing a sturdy white length of plastic with a buzzing ball at the end; she had seen this 'magic wand' in videos online, the few times she had snuck on to porn websites to indulge herself, and this presented the perfect opportunity to try it.

He held it there long enough for her to see it, then dropped it instantly between her rigid thighs and held it to her moist pussy.

She moaned deeply, the sound muffled only by the toy in her mouth. She couldn't believe it – the ball at the tip of the wand vibrated so fast that it felt like her lips and clitoris were being caressed and whipped and played with by a superhumanly fast expert. Her toes curled, and fingers clenched, muscles tightening through her like cables. She couldn't move, couldn't resist, open to Master's expert onslaught.

Maria thought of nothing but the now; her other life was a memory. She was here and now and vibrant and alive, a dutiful slave; but the truth was *she* was in charge. This is everything she wanted. To be worshipped and used, adored and abused, all at the same time.

The spinning stick brought her off again with a rasping cry; Master removed the dildo and let the sound escape and bounce around the cavernous chamber. Thick globules of saliva ran down its length and he dripped them onto her cheeks, now stained with rivulets of mascara. With thick fingers he worked the liquid across her skin, then squeezed her face roughly. Wheezing rasps hissed through her teeth as he flicked his tongue out and ran it across her smeared lips.

"You like this?" he whispered to her.

"I love it," Maria managed. "I love it."

He withdrew now with a stinging slap of her tits, leaving her there like a butterfly pinned behind glass, then returned to cover her eyes with one massive hand.

Pain spattered across Maria's red-flushed chest; tiny, fleeting stabs of white-hot pain, each one wresting a satisfied scream or sharp intake of breath. This is what she had demanded, what she wanted and it was all that she hoped it could be. When his hand came away she angled her head enough to see where the hot wet candle wax had hissed against fleshed and cooled in seconds, solidifying to form red flower-like brands across her. She was his now, his property, totally and truly.

He reached under her head to the bench and removed a bolt. The support behind Maria's head give way and swung down, adding a tension to her neck; she had to focus to keep her head lifted. As it rolled on her shoulder she felt blood rushing to it, clouding her vision, dulling her hearing. She watched Master approach upside down, the shameful stain she had left on his pants filling her view, then her mouth, the bulge of the mighty member within already hard for her, seeking entry. She tasted her own delightful juice on the fabric, jabbed her snaking, eager tongue at the material.

"Give it to me," she begged. "Give me your thick cock, I want it in me. Choke me again."

He unzipped and unsheathed it; nine inches, as thick as a bat, veins pulsing across it, all the way to its fat, purple head, an anaconda of fleshy authority.

"What do you want?" he asked.

"Fuck my face, fuck my throat."

"Beg."

"Please, Master. Use my mouth. I'm your good little slave."

"You are," he said with a seductive grin.

He clamped Maria's throat and angled her head backwards, lining up her gullet for perfect entry. He teased the pre-cum-slick, salty head against her hungry lips, the last traces of her lipstick leaving a claret stain on his head.

Then with zero subtlety or love, it was inside her. Its whole length plunged into her mouth, roughly, all the way to its thick root. Much bigger than the dildo, and far tastier. She was not sucking him, that was too easy; she was being fucked by him, her mouth a hole, her whole body an instrument he could use.

It was wonderful. The sound of her own throat catching, gagging. The feel of tears and spit running down her cheeks and spattering on the concrete. The sting of his palm as he brought it to her face, slapping his own cock through her skin. The candle wax he continued to drip, searing her in tiny droplets. The feel of his hands squeezing her wax-laced breasts. Being trussed here, completely unable to stop him.

He let her catch her breath. While she gulped down welcome lungfuls of air he unstrapped her, hauled her to her feet by her leash, turning her quickly and pushing her stomach to the bench, forcing her knees into small stirrups she hadn't noticed before. Her hands went back into the restraints and he secured her ankles once more.

He sat then and watched her; she could not see him, for his throne was behind her, but she knew, felt his eyes on her, taking in every inch. She had asked for this; to be viewed, to be interrogated.

"You're a slut who lost her way," the man told her. "You had dirty dreams and cocks lined up for you for the taking. For the fucking."

"I did," she whispered.

"You forgot how to be depraved. Forgot the beauty of the gutter, of letting yourself go, letting yourself be free, giving yourself to every desire."

"I did," she said, louder.

"You're trapped in an illusion of respectability. Your wear the everyday world like a cloak to hide your true self."

"I do!" she gasped. " I do, sir!"

"Are you a real slut?"

She was. She knew it, always had known it. Her desires were nothing to be ashamed of.

"I am!" she cried.

She heard his footsteps now. "Real sluts get all their lovely holes punished, don't they?" he said, circling her.

"Yes, Master, they do."

Maria could hear the rhythmic slap of something against flesh, and when he crossed her field of view she saw he was brandishing a new toy, a black dildo as thick as his cock. He went behind her, and she felt a warm trickle of saliva land between her splayed ass cheeks and course down across her puckered hole.

The wand snapped back to life and came to her cleft, bringing waves of intense pleasure back to her pussy; but that was secondary now to the feeling of a thick finger stirring between her buttocks, through the lube Master had provided, and pushing its way up to the knuckle into her ass.

"Oh yes, more," she pleased. "Take my ass. It's yours, sir."

Then came the toy, breaching her defenses, gaping the collar of her anus and sliding inside, dry, each piston-like motion a barb of pleasure and pain. Master lubed it up a little to allow it deeper, all the while holding the wand to her gossamer-laced, glistening quim. Muscular arms worked in perfect synchronicity, pleasuring both of her holes.

"I want yours!" she squealed as she approached orgasm.

The sensation of Maria's gaping ass closing quickly as the black dildo emerged was incredible, but not as wondrous as the feeling of his dick penetrating her with equal fervour; rubber was no substitute for flesh. The wand had gone but it had done its work, casting her off onto the road to coming again, and the sensation of Master's cock reaming her ass was all she needed now.

She screamed forcefully, knowing nobody could hear her but not caring either way, the noise drowning out the world save for the sound of her pulse pounding in her ears. The pressure reached crescendo, peaked, and she came violently with his rod in her ass, writhing in her bonds so that her wrists hurt. Another gush of her steaming ambrosia squirted from her slit, spraying onto Master's highly polished shoes.

He dismounted and came around, propping a foot onto the bench and allowing her tongue to lap up the juices she had tainted him with. If that was merely an aperitif, what followed was a meal; she could taste her sweet and naughty asshole on him. She was no longer alarmed at how turned on that made her feel.

"Incredible," she managed to say. "That was incredible."

He let out a cruel laugh. "Oh, my sexy little slut, we're not quite finished yet."

Of course they weren't; she knew that, because she had asked for all of this, but she was so sated, so alive and buzzing with the excitement of it, she would have happily ended it now.

No, she thought, *I would never turn down what comes next.*

Her prepared her for the final act with care, an aficionado of his craft, a collector preserving his most prized possession. He untied the straps slowly, deliberately, drawing her back to her feet. He peeled the hardened wax from her tits until she was clean, then produced from a pocket a shiny leather strap with a highly polished red plastic ball set into it.

Maria opened her mouth for him and the ball slid easily inside. He tightened it, gagging her, gifting her with silence, then kissed her forehead tenderly. She marveled at him as he made her slip her arms behind her back, each of his hands clutching her forearm, then he retrieved a further series of studded belts from beneath his throne and bound her arms.

Master brought out the clamps, two glistening silver clips at each end of a platinum chain. With care he applied them to her nipples; she had always wanted to try this and had never had the chance before. They were exquisite agony, pinching the brown buds of her tits, discomforting and energizing at the same time. He tugged playfully on the chain, bringing fresh ecstasy.

Then the harness came, lowering silently from the ceiling as if by magic, a firm cable extending off into the shadows above. It was all sturdy straps, buckles, steel rings and hooks, and once it was secured around her back and shoulders and knees, she was able to lean back, as if in a hammock, the harness taking her weight with ease. She felt the cable go taut, winched from some unknown source, and she was hoisted off the ground, a beautiful demon taking her first flight.

He span her and she twisted idly in the candle light, dizzying her a little. She felt adrift and yet safe, cocooned in this world of vice she had constructed for herself. When finally she stopped she saw Master held something else; a black rod of steel three feet long with a leather manacle at each end. These he secured around her booted ankles, the restraining bar ensuring her legs were spread wide and making her completely unable to move them closer together. With a deft movement he stepped under the bar into the triangle formed between her body and legs, fitting snugly between her tight, anticipant thighs, hulking cock bobbing in front of him.

He gripped Maria by her cinched waist with power and strength she had never known. His dark eyes fixed on hers, and would remain so for the entirety of the final act, savouring every twitch of her face, every roll of her eyes, every feeling of glee.

She managed an almost imperceptible nod.

He was in her seemingly without moving, occupying her, a welcome invading force, deeper than before, tilting her body in the harness as he worked a potent rhythm. What few moans she could make were lost in the darkness.

The flower of her pussy opened for him, gripped him with its sweet muscles, drawing him deeper. He licked his fingers and massaged the bud of her clitoris, playing with lips now ravaged by his attacks. Her desire to fend him off, to allow her fleeting respite, was impossible to sate with arms trussed against her spine, hanging there, helpless, a fucktoy, a true slut.

And she adored it, surrendered to it all.

His cock went from her hot-pink, soaking box to her ass, gaining easy entry to her tight canal thanks to her own natural lubrication. He dipped into her up to the hilt, his hips moving with machine-like precision. Their thighs mashed together, the slapping sound thunderous around them.

He alternated, fucking her ass for a few strokes then delving into her creamy pink slit, and back again, a single thrust to each, bouncing her encroaching orgasm from pillar to post.

The home stretch was to be in Maria's tender garden and she bore down with all her might, squeezing his cock with her inner walls, hoping it would melt into her, make them one, so she could remain here on the edge of ecstasy until time ceased to be. She held those dark eyes in her gaze, taking a mental image; her legs splayed and shackled behind him, her tits in bondage. She was unable to move or fight or do anything but be loved and worshipped for the goddess she was. As subservient as this scenario was she knew where the power lay.

Her orgasm blasted her wide open from within, a bomb ripping through nerves, destroying senses and memories as it consumed her. She was like a coiled spring unleashed, shooting for the heavens, all that energy released, propelling her skyward. She wanted forever to occupy that otherworldly place before gravity took over and she would drift to the ground.

Master withdrew and spun her cradle so her face was level with his cock. He exploded without a sound, his pleasure secondary to hers, shooting ropes of glistening cream across her mascara-black cheeks. It coated her ball gag and shot across her chin to pool in the hollow of her neck. She worked her lips around the plastic stopper to allow traces of his seed to roll inside her mouth, flicking her constricted tongue around to catch every salty, sweet drop.

He stood by her as she returned to earth, gently caressing her cheek, cleaning away his anointing gift. Her eyes were prickled with tears again, but of wonderful joy this time. She blinked them away and he unhooked the gag from the back of her head, letting her breathe, take in that first breath as if coming up from a deep, dark ocean. She smiled at him.

He released her and held her in his arms as the cable flew off into the dark. Like a god or saviour he unbound her by the light of the candles, caressed her, touched her, soothed her, peeled off her boots, rolled down her stockings, unzipped her from her corset. He stripped her bare.

Master's fingers went to the collar around Maria's neck and released her from it.

When she finally stepped back out into the daylight world she was changed.

She knew herself now, earnestly and joyously. With the help of a stranger, there in the darkness, she was found.

VANILLA
A Poem

"You're vanilla," he said,
His smirk an ugly truth,
Revealing himself, the gentlemanly veneer
Stripped away.

His mask was gone and she knew,
Certainly and endlessly,
He was not as kind as he acted,
Without experience, or poise, or charm.

He craved indulgence and thrills to
Cement the myth of him.
To do what the filth he spent so long worshiping
Had told him was the way.

"You're vanilla," he said as a bullet
Meant to wound, to hide his own deviance,
For he had no pride and too much shame,
To be free and open like she.

She who would do whatever felt right,
For the right soul, one who accepted
That there was no shame in wanting
To pleasure and be pleased.

"You're vanilla," he said, cold shoulder exposed,
Lying in his own sweat, from a frolic now forgotten,
Within seconds of its close,
Pedestrian and empty.

She did not give him a fraction of her everything,
He was undeserving and ironic,
Craving pornographic thrills and pallid emotions,
A hole to bury himself in.

PERFECT PLEASURES

"You're vanilla," she thought, and slipped away
To leave him dreaming of heartless sluts
And encounters that could never be,
Because he would hate all involved, himself most of all.

He was afraid of loving, exposing, being
Raw and stripped while still in clothes.
Her body was not the weapon he wanted,
But an instrument to be played and conducted.

"You're vanilla," she mused, his a thankless heart
That could never hit the right notes, of
Symphonies played out on skin and soul,
Flesh, bones and senses entwined.

She had composed an opus a day with her body
For those willing to listen, but he was deaf
To the sound of honesty and beauty and would be
Left to play solo without her.

"You're vanilla," she knew, because taboo
Was not a medal, a badge of honour to wear
As smutty armour in lieu of the understanding
Of sharing natural carnal joys.

He had no bragging rights, no stories,
Save for a final fumble with an angel now
And forever beyond his reach,
Off into the night with a spark in her heart.

"You're vanilla," she whispered as she left him behind,
To bare everything to one who would appreciate
What it was to share so fully that bodies
And minds had no limits.

Beyond depravity and shame, where the blur
Of rich flavours and heady sensation was sweet,
And satisfying and wholesome and true and
Words like vanilla meant nothing.

FOCUS

HE

We were going through one of the worst cold snaps I'd ever known, and the fact it was happening on the cusp of spring was even more annoying. Where there should have been sunshine and warmth there were grey days, ice and the kind of snowfall usually reserved for places closer to the poles.

Stephanie always saw the positives in everything, and the drifts outside were like an invitation to play. She put down whatever new book she was reading – an erotic novel, a genre with which she had become rather enamoured recently – and had that glimmer of mischief in her jade eyes. "Let's go for a walk," she suggested brightly.

I didn't take much convincing; sitting inside while the snow stacked up outside was like letting it gloat; it had already mucked our weekend plans to visit friends but it wouldn't hold us prisoner in our own home. Stephanie scurried away to dress as I turned away from the video I was editing – a promotional video for a local community centre desperate to rebrand itself – and pulled on my thick hiking boots and threaded my scarf around my neck.

She emerged from the bedroom all ready, peering out from the furry rim of her winter coat, green eyes sparkling beneath the band of her woollen beany hat. She flexed her fingers together to settle the leather gloves onto her hands. Beneath the visible sliver of a denim skirt she wore a pair of thick tights decorated with snowflakes that she had bought at Christmas but never worn. They looked fantastic on her, hugging her shapely legs all the way down to her knee high black leather boots.

I pulled on my own winter coat, begrudging the fact it was hanging on the rack and not bundled into the wardrobe as it should have been at this time of year, then my gloves. Within minutes we were outside, fastening coats as tight as they would go to keep out the chill.

Tiny snow particles drifted languidly on an icy breeze as we trudged out onto the road past great white mounds that flashed occasional strips of colour or showed off a protruding wing-mirror or antennae; anybody foolish enough to attempt to dig their car out of the growing drifts certainly wouldn't manage to drive it very far so few had tried. Tyre tracks along the road had filled swiftly, replaced with trails of footprints tracing uneven lines to their destinations.

"I love how everything changes when it snows," Stephanie said. "The roads and the paths go away and people just walk anywhere."

"That's awfully philosophical," I said.

"It is a bit, isn't it? Quick, draw a cock in the snow."

I took her hand and we walked, chatting idly, effortlessly, as we made our way towards the wood where we often walked after dinner. It was a series of paths weaving amongst trees, steps and slopes and streams, a quiet respite from the buzz of the city a mile away. It was a popular route for joggers and dog walkers, but today it was almost deserted. Aside from the occasional track of foot and paw prints the snow that had fallen along the public paths was unmarred and undisturbed, and as we moved further away from the suburban streets the quiet became absolute, serene and still in a winter landscape, broken only by the light crunch of our feet in the snow.

"This is lovely," Stephanie said, each sweet breath misting as it escaped her smiling pink lips. "Are you warm enough?"

"Just about," I said, rubbing my hands together, the friction doing little to bring additional heat to my digits.

"I'm a little too hot in this," Stephanie mused, and unbuttoned the toggle just below her throat. "That's better."

I glanced sideways and from my angle I could see inside her coat and the exposed peach flesh beneath. I let out a shocked gasp.

"Are you..."

"Am I what?"

"Are you topless under there?"

She skipped ahead and walked backwards before me, glancing around to ensure we were indeed alone. We may as well have been the only two people on the planet, and she quickly unbuttoned the next two latches and peeled the thick material back to expose herself.

Her pert breasts sat snugly against the fur lining of the coat, the cool air and her own excitement making tiny barbs of her brown nipples. I couldn't help but laugh, realising she had run off to the bedroom and stripped off her top as I'd been pulling on my coat. She was stunning, curls of red hair hanging from beneath her woollen hat, lips curved in a playful smile as she exposed her breasts to me, giggling at her own naughtiness. It made my heart soar, and I loved her so fiercely in that moment, adored her playful spirit, her sense of adventure, propriety be damned.

"You and those damned books..." The story she had been reading had no doubt given her the idea to do this, and I made a mental note to thank the writer should our paths ever cross. Flakes of snow peppered her goosepimpled skin and she snapped the coat shut again, shivering in delight. "They bring out something wild in you..."

"You love it," she said, still backstepping but slowing down so I could catch up with her. I put my hands on her hips and pulled her close. Her crotch grinded against mine, coaxing my loins to stir as she had done so on countless occasions. The faint smell of her perfume and the taste of cherry lip balm soothed me as our lips met, and her eager tongue slipped its way into my mouth, a sure fire way of getting my full attention below the belt.

"I do," I breathed. "What's the friskiest thing you've ever done in the snow?"

"Snowball fight," she joked, and I laughed into the crook of her neck, looking into the folds of her coat to see the swell of her cleavage. "No, it was really kinky. Unprotected. I didn't wear gloves!"

I peeled back the layers of the coat to expose her again, right there on the footpath, our own private slice of the outside world, and cupped her breasts with my gloved hands, flexing my fingers into the supple flesh.

"I was hoping to make the number one today," Stephanie said, sweet breath foggy in the chill. I kissed her again, hungrily, and with another wary glance around I lowered my head, flicking my tongue over her icy skin, the raised brown flesh of her areola a textured artwork beneath my careful nurture.

"It's a plan," I said, pinching her nipples between my teeth the way I knew she loved. She squeaked with glee and I pressed my luck, nipping tighter until she gave a small but stern slap with her leather gloved fingers. The blow was raw against my skin so I seethed and pulled away. My angel withdrew from me, her bare breasts a lure I could never resist; she led me a few feet off the main path to a small grove amongst snow-laden bushes, leaning against the frosty bark of a gnarled tree. It towered over us with its brethren, branches drooping beneath the weight of the snow.

She arched her back against the wood, breasts thrust out towards me and I cupped them once more, nestling my face between their ample warmth. Stephanie loved her breasts being played with in every way, kissed, licked and sucked and I obliged her desires as I always did. Her hand tickled my neck and slid through my tousled hair and she gasped and tittered with every motion.

"You must be so cold," I said, rolling my tongue against the stiff bullets of her nips.

"Just so turned on," she trilled, and took my hand and pushed it between her legs. Her short denim skirt rolled up across her spread thighs and my wool-clad fingers pushed against the undercurve of her body; I could feel so little and withdrew my hand. "Let me."

I put a fingertip to her mouth and her teeth pinched the material over my index finger. With a whip of her neck she took the glove off and spat it away. My fingers quickly returned to their destination, warmed immediately by the heat radiating from her. I circled the thick denier material and sensed instantly the moisture that had soaked through.

She wasn't wearing panties.

Stephanie watched my reaction and smiled when my face split with a shocked grin. "Oh, Steph..."

"Always be prepared," she said as I massaged the folds of her moistening snatch through the stitching, pushing it delicately into the shallow pool of her spreading joy. I honed in on her clit, circling it, still suckling at her nipples. I maintained eye contact throughout, just the way she loved; made her feel like the only soul on the planet I would ever love and pleasure in this way. She stroked my cheek, puffing hot breaths in synch with every flick of my fingers.

I sucked in those escaping clouds as we kissed hungrily. My bare digits felt the cold and sought warmth, diving beyond the elastic waistband of her tights and sliding against her flesh until they found her supple channel. I rolled against her swollen clit and she mewled in my ear. My middle and forefinger split and skated down her labia, skating the surface of her wetness.

Stephanie's hips bucked, wanting me deeper. I moved my hand to her throat and clutched her bare flesh in a motion that was both gentle and firm and held her gaze as I sank deeper, curling them against her, vanishing into her like they were being drawn by her own gravity. She pursed her lips and breathed a slow breath, her thigh muscles vibrating. Those knee high boots held.

I knew every inch of her body; we are more compatible than we'd been with any other partner either of us had ever been with. Those first months of our relationship had been spent in beautiful exploration of each other's pleasures, passions and erogenous hotspots. I knew the precise location of her internal joy and stroked the pads of two fingers against it, a conductor orchestrating the symphony of her delight. The tremulous cry started in her chest, low and breathy and echoing out of her open mouth as sound and mist.

She held the back of my neck and rode my hand. I never looked away from her eyes. She was mine and I hers, and it would always be this way. We were responsible for each other. Our safety, wellbeing, emotions and joy were dependent on the other and we would tend to each others needs until the sun burned out. I guided her to her own supernova and her eyes widened, rolled and grew momentarily distant, lids fluttering as she came with a seething, barely controlled rasp. She hung off me until her orgasm subsided then relaxed against the tree bark, the flushed-red flesh of her chest heaving, the swell of her bosom a beautiful, hypnotic delight

"Oh, I love you. I adore every inch of you," I said, sliding my fingers free. I held them between our faces. They were coated with her musky moisture and as the icy air assaulted them the residual heat turned to steam and drifted from those digits like smoke.

Stephanie took my wrist and directed my fingers to my mouth, delighted as I sucked her essence from them. Hers was a fresh and tangy taste that I never got tired of, and I cleaned every last trace of that delicacy from my hand.

With nobody else but us within sight or earshot, Stephanie gripped me by the lapels and span me with feral strength, forcing me back against the same tree. Her hands sought my belt, unclasping and unzipping my trousers with amazing speed. She smiled her temptress' smile and watched every reaction: the expectant anticipation, the sharp intake of breath as she exposed my engorged tool to the cold, the biting of my lower lip as she clasped it. I love the feeling of textured material or leather against me as much as I do bare flesh, and the gloves made an incredible difference, lukewarm and creasing as she ensnared the seven inches of hard meat she had devoted countless hours to.

She steered the swollen head of my cock against the chill flesh of her chest, circling her nipples. I made no demands of her, letting her lead, steer my pleasure by that most potent of rudders. My balls were tight against me, a mix of the subzero temperature and sheer thrill.

"Someone's excited..." she said in a sing-song voice, and checked around us once more to ensure we were alone. She waited until I mirrored her action and searched for stunned onlookers, and the second I was distracted she slid her steaming mouth over my length all the way to the base.

Bliss. Pure and simple. The delight of the warmth around my prick was total and I couldn't keep in my excitement. I gasped and laughed at the same time, like the giddiest of school boys; my first experience of this act had been mind-blowing only insofar as it had been unprecedented and desired for so long, but my raging hormones had ended it no sooner than it had begun. Now I had more stamina, but I was so aroused at being fellated with such fervour, and in public no less, that I could easily see hitting my peak within seconds. My one gloved hand clutched at cold, rough bark as if to hold on for dear life; my exposed hand found the back of her head, fingers stroking the wool of her beanie and the vines of flame-red hair that spilled out. Her green eyes never left mine as her tongue tickled my most intimate flesh, whipping against tender skin as she bobbed back and forth. I fell in love with her all over again, as I did every time she went down on me. Every time she allowed me the privilege of touching her. Of loving her.

Stephanie broke contact, her cheeks raw and rosy with the chill, and she laughed her most wicked, dirty laugh, deep and throaty. "You should see your face."

"Can you really blame me?" I breathed as she ran the tip of her tongue down the underside of my cock, lapping at my tight scrotum, lowering my prick to drag her tongue back to the tip across the upper side. She brought another hand to help and pumped me back and forth as she watched me with those swirling jade orbs set into that goddesses' visage.

"How can we melt this hard icicle?" she wondered.

"Temperature puns? Really, that's where we're at? Don't cheapen this."

She rose, sliding up my body, trapping my dick between my own flesh and the exposed wall of her stomach. My balls brushed against the moist gusset of her tights and I twitched. She shoved me aside with a cackle and pivoted at the waist so her shoulder rested against the tree, and I shuffled back to watch her leather-wrapped fingers lift up her coat and expose the full roundness of her ass beneath the wool tights. She unveiled her pale buttocks like the greatest prize on the world's best game show, and I swore I could see the faint mist of condensing heat glimmer between her thighs, drift up between the canyon of her cheeks and away into the ether.

"How cheap am I now?"

"Still way out of my price range," I said, and I meant it. I have always felt unworthy of her. Mere mortals shouldn't be permitted such heavenly delights as this. Yet here she was, inviting me in from the cold to warm myself at her most blistering altar. How could I refuse?

I clutched her hips with my mismatched hands and guided myself in, relishing the heat that radiated from her as I approached. She held the sturdy, age-old presence of the tree for stability and mewled as I played the saliva-slick head of my dick through her wet furrow. The bunched material of her tights squeezed at her thighs and my balls brushed against it, heightening the sensation as I finally sought entry.

It was like dipping into molten steel. My whole body caught fire and both of us gasped as we shared primal body heat in the winter landscape. I leaned over her to kiss the exposed flesh of her neck and held there, sealed inside her scalding moisture and never wishing to leave.

"I love you..." I said softly, and she responded by thrusting my hips back, bucking me half way out of her and forcing me to thrust back quickly to return to her warmth. She laughed huskily.

"Are you waiting for another invitation like that?"

I slipped in again with a measured but forceful stroke and worked up a rhythm. I breathed in the heady scent of her perfume once more, nuzzled her coils of copper hair. My hands slipped round to cup her breasts, her nipple scratching the bare skin of one hand and scoring the thick glove of the other. I squeezed and massaged in time with my thrusts. She angled her head to kiss me and our steaming breath was a single, unified cloud.

I don't know what came over me then. Perhaps it was the rawness of the situation, a greedy need for more, or perhaps a strange connection with nature since we were so openly brazen, as if societal rules had yet to be applied. But I swept my arms around her, slipped free of her and drew her straight to the ground. We fell side by side and the snow gathered between us. Her eyes widened and mouth fell open in shock. She yelped and beat my forearms against my chest. I pulled her close and the veil of snow between us melted beneath the pressure.

"I love you too, but I'm going to kill you," she gasped, and I rolled her onto her back and bridged my legs either side of her, tugging her tights lower so her cheeks and thighs nestled into the stinging snow. Every sensation made us feel more alive.

I slipped off her hat and teased out her hair across the faultless plain of the snow. It was wildfire igniting, red and orange paint spreading across a blank canvas,. I kissed her then as if I hadn't done it before and she pulled me closer, sucking my tongue into her mouth, devouring me with hunger.

I entered her again, tight within the walls of her quim. Every shiver that swept through her transferred straight to me and we trembled together in a mix of plunging temperature and vibrant desire. The heat and pressure around my cock was so intense, I wanted to burrow deeper, and her gloved hands clutching my backside encouraged me to quicken my thrusts. The mountains of her tits heaved against my buttoned coat, nipples alert and tender, the gooseflesh across her chest bristling with crimson as an orgasm approached. I could see it in her eyes, those whirlpools of jade into which I could tumble forever, and seeing her crest the edge of her orgasm brought on mine without delay.

"I can't hold back..."

"I wouldn't expect you to..." she seethed through gritted teeth. I gasped openly. Her mouth curled in delight as I came; she felt my deluge, contracted and took everything I had to offer. I fell against her and she cradled me in her arms as the last drop of my essence seeped into her core. Her breathing rang in my ears along with the thundering of my pulse.

I caught my breath just as Stephanie held hers and clutched me tighter, and when I looked up I saw through the gnarled branches of a tree not ten feet away we were being watched.

A woman in a fur coat peered at us from behind a thick tree trunk, and beside her was a man in a hearty winter jacket. They wore scarves and boots. They were somewhere in their late forties. As soon as we clocked eyes on them they withdrew back behind the tree.

"What do we do now?" Stephanie whispered, frozen beneath me.

"I don't know. I don't think we really have any right to be embarrassed or accuse them of spying..."

I slipped free and zipped my manhood back out of site, quickly helping Stephanie to her unsteady feet. She pulled up her tights, fastened her coat and patted the snowflakes from her clothing, swept her hair back beneath her hat somewhat haphazardly so half of her auburn locks hung across her shoulder. It was as if nothing had happened, but we had been caught in the act. Stephanie's cheeks burned as red as her hair.

"Brave face," I said, and I took her hand, leading her back out on to the main path where the couple had no doubt been walking when they had seen us. That they had stopped to watch said they were clearly less prudish than perhaps we were giving them credit for, and we hadn't seen them bolt off in the opposite direction just yet.

Sure enough, there they were still, hiding behind the tree, clutching on to each other in their embarrassment at being caught watching. The issue of moral high ground was dubious here. I couldn't help but wave my free hand and said, in my best approximation of nonchalance: "Afternoon."

"Hello there," the woman said, and I could see how flushed her cheeks were. She was attractive and her accent was somewhat refined, though I imagined she was affecting that to seem above the situation. "Lovely day."

"It is," I agreed. "Perfect for..."

Stephanie was quick to leap in and save the awkward silence.

"Making snow angels!"

"Snow angels, right," the voyeuristic gentleman said, nodding his head in agreement. "I'm sure they...were fantastic."

"Yes, lots of fun," Stephanie said quickly and steered me away from the conversation, tugging me gently along the path.

"Have a nice day," I said, and we scurried away with as much of our dignity as we could muster. "That was close..."

"Close?" Stephanie giggled. "Close? Any closer and they'd have joined in! Come on, let's get inside before we cause a scandal."

We hurried away, but seconds later we heard the sound of feet crunching snow and turned to see the gentleman who had spied on us jogging up the path. His wife was further behind him, walking slowly. He had something in his hand and he lifted it for us to see.

"You forgot your glove," he said with a knowing smile, and I took it with a bashful grin.

"Thank you, sir," I said brusquely. "Much appreciated."

I made a move to usher Stephanie away, but the gentleman wasn't finished.

"Before you go," he said, and he tarried long enough for his wife to catch up, allowing us a good look at them. They were perhaps fifteen years our senior, and I'd place them at around forty-five, but both had a youthful zest in their eyes and skin; watching a live sex show on a snowy spring day clearly agreed with them. I knew somehow they were in excellent shape, lithe bodies apparent even beneath their thick winter wrappings.

The embarrassment we were feeling was tempered with curiosity; what in the hell could these people want, and be so insistent on holding us here for a chat as to forego their own feelings of awkwardness?

"So...how's business?" the gentleman said, and I shuffled my feet to gather snow either side of my boots.

"It's...great?" I ventured. "We really have to go..."

The wife nudged her husband in the ribs and he gave an *oof* even despite the layers of protective material. "He doesn't remember, Simon. Forgive me if we can't remember your name, and I'm sure you don't remember ours, but we secured your services about a year ago. A music video for our son... The band was called *Cleopatra's Corset*."

The cogs of memory ratcheted the recollection into focus, and I remembered a four-piece comprising teenagers playing at being at cool, thrashing out middling rock across a variety of locations; a garage, a local pub, and incongruously on the shore, where we'd struggled to get the shots they'd asked for before the tide came in. His parents, standing before me, had paid for it all as an eighteenth birthday gift, and I knew they were in shape because I remember being in their kitchen when they had returned from mutual gym session and run, bodies sheened with sweat in the summer light.

The job had been easy and swift, and I'd been a journeyman shooting what I was paid for and had edited it together with their demo overlaid, crafting the epitome of a clichéd music promo for a teenage rock band I doubted would go the distance.

"Oh yes!" I said brightly, and mustered as much professionalism as I could when face to face with a couple who've previously paid you money for services and have also seen your penis. "Of course I remember, that was a fun shoot. How are the band doing?"

"Oh, they broke up," the woman said with a dismissive wave. "They were terrible."

I didn't comment. I still couldn't remember their names, but I remember our encounters being easy and professional, a far cry from what was happening here. Stephanie swayed beside me, arm brushing mine almost imperceptibly but I took it as a sign that she wanted to head back home with whatever dignity she still held.

"Well, it's nice to see you again," I said smoothly, and my freelancer's brain overwrote the idiot setting and I added: "And keep me in mind if you have any more video work that needs doing."

The couple looked at each other with lopsided grins. "Well, funny you should mention that…"

*

I was looking at the phone number and the address that Simon Jenson had scrawled on the back of my business card as Stephanie laid a steaming mug of coffee on the table beside me; it plumed delicious mist into the air, and would shun the last of the cold from our bones, though our exertions had already seen to that. She sipped from her own mug and looked at the card.

She nudged her elbow against my shoulder. "Well, what the hell are you waiting for, Rich?"

Simon and Eleanor had been suitably vague about their desires for their new video, but I had a feeling I knew precisely what they were after. They had gone so far as to invite us around to their home – a ten minute walk from our own – this evening to discuss precisely what they wanted. They would wine and dine the both of us, for they had insisted Stephanie come along too, and if I wasn't prepared to take on the job, then there would be no hard feelings.

"Isn't it a little...awkward?" I mused.

Stephanie, ever-adventurous, took the card and rolled it between her nimble fingers. "What happened earlier was awkward. This is...kind of exciting, don't you think? And hey...it's *work*... We're not exactly in a climate where we can go turning down too many paying jobs."

"You're hitting me with business sense when a couple's probably going to ask us to video them screwing?" The next thought hadn't occurred to me until now. "And possibly join in...?"

"Forget that," she said. She bit her lower lip in the way that she always did when arousal struck, and I could see the glimmer in her eyes that she at least wanted to investigate this further.

It is a curse that I find it impossible to say no to her.

SHE

The snow made it a risk and a chore to drive so we opted to walk, wrapping up warm for the second time that day. We took a shortcut through the park, passing the area where we had loved and been caught earlier in the afternoon; there had been some light flurries of snowfall but the signs of our lust were still there. Richard clutched me tightly.

"I can't believe we did that," he said. "I can't believe we're doing this."

"Come on, where's your sense of adventure?" I said, slapping his rump and rushing on ahead.

We reached a large detached house on a quiet avenue lined with snowdrifted cars and overhanging trees bending beneath the weight of white. We walked up the driveway past the garage in which Rich had filmed the band, past the bay window spilling a bright yellow glow, reached the door and knocked.

Simon Jenson answered, clad in a smart charcoal grey shirt and dark jeans, and I knew Rich would be glad that his outfit of a blue shirt and chinos matched a similar smart-casual style; he had fretted about being too dressed up or not dressed up enough when selecting his clothes.

"Good evening," Simon beamed. "Come in, come in."

I let Rich usher me inside and Simon took my jacket, revealing the polka dot blouse and knee-length pleated skirt that never failed to make me feel beautiful. Thick black tights – a pair that lacked the snowflakes that had adorned me earlier – and boots completed the ensemble and I looked like a latter-day pinup girl. I flashed Rich a quick smile, and I saw in his eyes his love and desire for me. It made me feel rich and complete. He took off his coat and slipped his arm around my waist to reassure me. I felt protected and safe.

Simon gave a quick tour of the ground floor as we headed to the kitchen; a living room decked out in rich burgundy and oak furniture, with an open, natural coal fire place, currently extinguished, but I had no doubt it would be incredible and inviting when burning; a spacious dining room with beautiful light fixtures and minimalist art adorning the walls; a library/study area with shelves overflowing with books of all sizes and genres and chaise lounges for sprawling during reading time, the sight of which brought sparks of longing and envy into my heart. I loved my books, and craved a library like this.

We followed the sound of classic 70s rock and the scent of a baking lasagne through to the kitchen, where Eleanor Jenson, in an elegant floral dress that clung tightly to her narrow frame, was preparing salad as the meal cooked in the glowing orange window by her exposed knees. She grinned.

"So glad you could come," she said. "Dinner won't be long. Red or white?"

"Red," Rchard and I said in unison.

Simon poured us deep glasses of a shiraz that warmed us through to the core, and we made small talk with nary a mention of what they had seen us do this afternoon, or why we had been invited around this evening. We asked them about work; he was a department head for a telecommunications company, she an accountant, and they both talked positively of experiences but how work was just a means to an end. We said much the same; Rich's freelancing in videography and new media had its ups and downs but was treating us well at the moment, and my job as an area manager for a chain of fashion stores was certainly a benefit to us. Much like the Jensons, neither of us lived to work, merely worked to live, as well as we possibly could. I liked these people; they were easy going and disarmingly charming at every turn, and I could see that Rich felt the same.

The lasagne and home-made garlic bread was amongst the finest either of us had ever tasted, and accompanied by the wine and the easy conversation, it was easy to forget that we had met – or met again, in Richard's case – through something rather uncivilised. They made no suggestive jokes or crude snipes. When I was certain I couldn't have liked them more, Eleanor's homemade black forest gateau came along to prove me wrong.

"Let us wash up, it's the least we can do," Rich insisted as we cleaned our plates and pushed them to the centre of the table.

"You'll do no such thing," Eleanor insisted, stacking the plates and ferrying them into the kitchen and returned, shutting the door behind her. "That's a job for tomorrow and we'll hear no more about it."

They invited us through to the living room where we sank into a plush sofa with our refilled wine glasses, and our hosts sat on the adjacent seating, and I couldn't quell a smile as their fingers interlaced together and a mutual blush swept over their cheeks.

"Now then, I suppose the time has come to talk business," Simon said with an awkward, lopsided grin that was a mixture of embarrassment and excitement. Eleanor mirrored it, and I found myself liking them just that little bit more. They were *good* together. They were one of those couples that just fit. They had been together for enough years to be totally at ease with one another, and I hoped that Rich and I, when that much time had been shared between us, would be the same. Easy, at peace and very much in love. "We'd like to procure your services, Richard, as a videographer for a private project of a...rather personal nature."

"We would," Eleanor agreed bashfully, and then her eyes widened as if struck by a mortified realisation. "And I just want to add that this isn't a seedy invite to be part of an orgy or a swinging foursome or anything like that. We didn't invite you here to disrespect you in that way."

I laughed, and Rich laughed harder, at how cute the older woman was when so flustered, but there was some relief there that we hadn't been led here under the illusion of a job then propositioned for more. With Richard, we had done most things in our time together. We had worked our way through the karma sutra and re-enacted porn scenarios as they played out on the TV before us; we had roleplayed doctors and nurses, teachers and students, prison officer and inmate, and countless other scenes. We had loved each other on the beach, in alleyways behind clubs, in the back of a taxi; we had handcuffed, spanked and whipped each other; we had pretended to be strangers in hotel bars and fucked the night away as if we had never met and never would again. We had been tender, and rough, and wild, and every stage in between. But I knew, more certainly than anything else, that as adventurous as we were, I couldn't bear to share him, and I knew he felt the same.

"Don't worry, it hasn't crossed my mind," Rich said. "Well, maybe a bit, but it's reassuring."

"Not that you're both not incredibly beautiful and handsome and what-have-you," I said, instinctively covering for whatever implication Richard may have inadvertently made, and made the blushing and giggling spread. "Be quiet, Stephanie." I clapped my hands together resolutely. "So, anyway. Sex tape!"

The Jensons guffawed. "Well, that's what it boils down to, I suppose," Simon agreed.

"We'd just like something a little more elegant than the usual," Eleanor added, cringing at a memory. "We tried sticking a camera at the foot of the bed and shot some awful amateur porn. Badly lit, badly framed. It was bad. Bad!"

I perked up, embarrassment forgotten. "Oh, we did that too, it was *awful!*"

"I thought I did okay..." Richard said, affecting an arrow through the heart.

"You were fabulous," I reassured with a roll of my eyes. "But it was just the latest in a long line of terrible amateur smut shot the world over."

Eleanor slapped Simon's shoulder. "See, I'm not the only one. It needs to have some *style*."

My memory twitched, and I remembered the murky fog of a drunken encounter after an evening in our favourite wine bar, when we had returned home, donned masks and gone onto a webcam chat site and performed on demand for distant, anonymous strangers. I leaned forward conspiratorially, the wine loosening my lips and inhibitions in glorious fashion. "One time, we even went into a webcam room with masquerade masks on and did it for an audience."

"Oh, we'll have to try that one," Eleanor said, eyes lighting up with possibilities.

"It's not classy but it's a kick."

"We want both," Simon explained. "The class and the kick. A little production value. Something romantic and beautiful, naughty and nice."

"Something we can look back on in years to come and say - " and Eleanor counted them off on her fingers as she spoke – "One, we did something wild. Two, we were in great shape, for two people in their mid forties. Three, we were *good*..." She looked around the house, at the family portraits adorning the walls. "We had kids young. *Really* young, and we never really got a chance to be *wild*. Now the kids are off to Uni, and it's just us and..."

"We feel like we have some catching up to you," Simon conceded, stroking Eleanor's knee in a perfect blend of passion, affection and friendship. "Seeing you two today, you're the us twenty years ago that never quite got a chance to do that sort of thing. Well, kind of...we did do it in that cave on the beach, remember?"

His wife giggled winsomely. "That dog-walker got quite the eyeful!"

I clapped my hands together in excitement. "I get it. I totally get it. It's beautiful."

"We'd like both of you to do it," Eleanor added, "If that's okay? It balances it out, and there'll be no secrets between you two. And we rather like the idea of being watched by a couple who are so passionate."

I looked at Rich, knowing he would need my approval. I had no hesitation in me, only delight at the notion of being involved. The thought of the scenario was taking delicious root inside my brain; I wanted to be a part of it.

"I'd be honoured," I said with a sultry smile, and a squeeze of Richard's hand.

"It seems we have ourselves a deal," he said, and the Jensons swelled with relief and excitement.

"Marvelous," Eleanor giggled, fingers tapping against her husband's thigh. "How does tomorrow suit you?"

*

I fled through the crisp darkness with my lover in pursuit, desperate to stay ahead to prolong this game but craving to be caught, dragged into the snow where I'd been ravaged earlier and taken all over again. His fingers brushed my clothes, nipped at my flesh through the heavy layers, and I realised he was constantly staying a step behind; he could have caught me whenever he wanted, but he wanted the game to last just as I did. To nip and grope and tease, to prime me for release as soon as we got home, but I had other plans. There was research to be done.

We reached our front door and I fumbled my key in the lock as he pressed himself against me from behind; through the layers I felt his swollen lust nudge against my buttocks and I reached back to squeeze it. His hot breath puffed into my periphery.

"I hope I'm not the only one thrilled at the idea of what we're going to do tomorrow," he said.

"I can't wait," I said, and it was the certain truth. I wanted to be part of something so wonderfully intimate yet overwhelmingly voyeuristic. Making love outdoors today was a buzz, but knowing that we had been watched for a part of it made my knickers moisten at the mere recollection. I squirmed as Rich's fingers circled my waist and delved between the buttons of my coat, seeking the radiating warmth.

I opened the lock and we spilled clumsily into the hall. The door latched behind us and Rich had me against the wall no sooner than I had flicked on the light. My coat came off and I made an attempt to kick off my boots, flailed like a lunatic until Rich dropped to his knees like a true gentleman and plucked them from my feet. He held my bare heel against his shoulder and slid his hand up my inner thigh, homing in on me with intent to pleasure.

I slapped the hand away and scurried into the living room to where we had left the laptop on. I nudged the mouse to wake it from sleep, and he was already peeling my dress from my shoulders. The warm flat soothed my chill flesh, and the goosebumps that were quelled by the heat were brought back instantly by the feel of his tongue tracing down my back. His hands circled me and through the material of my bra he tweaked my nipples. I stuck to my task and called up a window, typing in the address of a streaming video site we'd been known to frequent when the mood struck.

I like porn, and occasionally love it, if it inhabits the right territory, but it so rarely hits the spot. So much turned me off, like the banal, sweatless gonzo of the casting couch and the overly aggressive rawness that made out things like throatfucking and fisting were everyday events. The clichéd cringefests of porn-scene setup that saw doctors and nurses rutting on the operating table, or plumbers moonlighting as gigolos to service the needs of housewives who'd always conveniently dressed up for the occasion. While I could be tempted and enthralled by these things, it wasn't often. I craved more from my smut, and what we were doing tomorrow, I felt oddly responsible for, perhaps more so than the expert currently stripping me naked. It had to be *good*.

So... to the competition...

Two dozen thumbnails loaded, tiny screen grabs of a variety of debauched acts. Bare flesh, interlocking bodies. Exposed tits, spread legs. Fat cocks sinking into tight, wet pussies and assholes; this was the language of porn and the titles all mirrored the content with the creative bankruptcy of immediate need. Everything was specifically categorised and coded based on difference and exclusivity: 'Asian Lesbians Dildo Fuck Latina Pussy'; 'Extreme Creampie'; '7 Men Cum In A 19 Year Old Cunt'.

I picked one at random whose title proclaimed with comparative restraint 'Slut Gets Railed' and the page refreshed to depict a buffering video with no preamble; a girl in knee-high boots was bent over a coffee table while a man gifted her with a length that could have collapsed marble columns with a robust swing. It slipped into her and she made a noise like an army of seals being clubbed in unison. The man it belonged to hefted it within her with a verve that bordered on psychotic, and the camera framing dutch-angled in on it in an HD closeup that almost burned my eyeballs out.

It came closer as Rich pushed with measured force against my upper spine and bent me over the table, slipping my panties down across my hips so I was completely bare and lit by the glow of a laptop screen.

"It's so impersonal and empty sometimes," I managed, and breathed quietly as Rich clamped his mouth around me. His tongue slithered past my wet lips and dipped to tickle my clit. My knees knocked together and my legs trembled. He flattened me against the cold glass of the table and he raised his head to peer at the screen over the arch of my buttocks.

"It has a place," he said between sucking mouthfuls of my essence. "It's rough and raw and graphic to the point of..."

Rich was disinclined to finish his sentence, and I was flattered that the taste of my nethers was enough of a distraction. I clicked back to the main page and sought a menu that listed specific categories that divided sex into specifics and fetishes and limiting, thoughtless fucks. Cumshots, black & ebony, squirting, swingers and teens. Surgically augmented and heavily made-up maidens writhed and bucked and sucked with men with dicks the likes of which would likely require an extra weight allowance to go through customs. Fetishes I couldn't fathom were played out and waiting for me to click the right place, and anything that wasn't represented professionally was supplied by budding amateurs with their own video cameras and basic editing facilities.

There was something wonderfully intense about seeing such vulgar snapshots while Richard's skilled tongue swept me towards an orgasm, and I gasped gently as he ate, a far cry from the caterwauling that seeped from the tinny computer speakers. So few of the orgasms I'd seen in porn were real, or at least if they were they were exaggerated out of all proportion.

Mine came with an intense tightness and a dizzying headrush; I gripped the edge of the table as my lips quivered beneath the pressure of his, mewling and gasping in delight. My hand skidded with the mouse and sought the category in the list I always preferred, and as my orgasm faded I clicked the 'Female Friendly' tag. Richard rose behind me, kissing each nodule of spine on the way to my neck, and I giggled and growled at the back of my throat as his teeth nipped my flesh. His hand covered mine and guided the mouse to a video entitled 'Fiery Passion.' The thumbnail depicted a slender, perky breasted redhead straddling a buff gentleman on clean white sheets.

We clicked together, and at the same time Richard entered me with slow and tender relish, burying himself into me inexorably as the video buffered and began. There was no setup, no plot, in much the same way the first video had none, but there was a romantic air to this video that the other sorely lacked. The camera was either static with carefully composed shots, or moved slowly in easy panning motions across the frame as the two participants lost themselves to each other. The camera shifted focus, blurring the foreground, casting moments and shapes into crisp relief, intensifying the experience, drawing us in.

The handsome gentleman performed oral the way Rich did, with total devotion, and when she returned the favour it was soothingly, tenderly and wholly. She sucked him deeply and slathered him with attention, but it never felt gratuitous. When finally he entered her they moved with lithe, discreet and muscular undulations; it was physical but not trying too hard, and they rarely broke eye contact throughout the changes in position. This was real sex as much as it was porn. Real physicality, real bodies fusing together. The sounds were delicate, breathy, and the occasional screech felt real and earned. The couples were sweating, and the redhead's chest was flushed a genuine tell-tale red.

"This is it..." Richard said. "This is what it has to be."

We watched it all, twenty odd minutes, and throughout it all he was within me, moving us inexorably towards climax, with the natural abandon of real and passionate love. He breathed in my ear, nibbled my lobe, caressed my hair and kissed my neck, his chest forever bonded to my back.

I held my orgasm at bay for as long as possible; I wanted us to come in unison with each other and the lovers on the display before us. Their rhythm increased with the urgency of the impending upsurge, and ours followed suit.

We came, two bodies in the here and now synchronised with a climax had an unknowable time ago and echoing digitally from around the world. Richard's come gushed into me and I moaned at the sensation I utterly adored.

He slipped from me as the video ended and pulled the laptop closed, and with chivalry that made my heart flutter he swept me into his arms and carried me through the bedroom, lay us down together and cradled me as we drifted off to sleep to dream of what we would do tomorrow.

*

Without script or storyboard, Simon and Eleanor loved each other before our lenses, and it did not take long for it to feel as if they had forgotten we were there. By the glow of the firelight, there were no cuts, no pauses, no second takes. Their bodies undulated and interlocked in a beautiful display of sweat-sheened limbs. We kept our distance and let them play; I knew Richard's camera would stay wide, capturing the full glory of their lust and love for each other. Every close up was carefully framed to show the intimacy, and I could barely take my camera from their faces, preserving every bite of the lip, every kiss, every uncontrollable gasp or hiss or roll of the eyes. I was obsessed with capturing every exquisite reaction. The Jensons never once looked at the camera, but held their attention on each other, until they erupted in a final, beautiful peak.

They collapsed, and kissed, and caressed, and I needed that intimacy again, I craved this experience more than any other.

"I want to shoot a film of our own," I said softly, and Richard's face brightened with a sinful smile.

"I was hoping you'd say that."

From beneath the thick sheepskin quilt, the Jensons broke their kiss and chuckled. Eleanor purred: "We thought you'd never ask."

The next evening, they returned the favour, and we both ended up with a document more personal and intimate than anything we could have made on our own, preserving such intense beauty for all eternity.

But I wasn't quite done. The erotic books I read demanded attention alongside the visual and aural experience. I wanted, *needed* us to write about it all, to tell our tale jointly, to arouse the mind as well as the eyes and ears. We worked on it together, side by side, writing our accounts and binding them as one. For inspiration we would throw on the videos we had been a part of; that of the strangers who had become friends and had invited us to share in their passions, and that of ourselves, lost in each other as the camera rolled. Erotica, pornography, sexuality and love entwined in a tapestry across mediums until we had told our story.

"How do we finish it?" I asked him, when we were close to completion, and my sex thrummed and ached for the contact I knew he would give me in just a few seconds.

That smile, that damned smile that made my heart thunder every time, appeared on the face that I loved more than any other, and I knew it was there because he felt the same way. He ran a hand up my forearm and tickled the exposed flesh at my neck.

"To be continued..."

THE MADISON BANQUET

1

Hannah lifted a foot above the surface of the steaming water, watching rivulets rush down the pale skin of her shapely toes, calve and thigh and return to the mass her body was submerged in, hidden beneath the veil of bubbles. In the hour she had spent within these chambers she had come to love them, this bathroom in particular; the freestanding tub fed through brass pipes buried beneath the marble floor; the ornate, wrought-iron candelabras that bathed the entire room in a soothing orange glow; the ambient music piped in from hidden speakers as if entering this realm from the beyond; and the huge mirrors that took up the entire adjacent walls, giving the room the illusion of stretching off to infinity where a thousand replicas of herself washed with the scented oils and expensive soaps, reclining in her own personal paradise. This room itself was bigger than her own bedroom at home, a world away from the luscious decadence she now enjoyed.

The Madisons had insisted.

They were still very much an enigma to Hannah, and she had seen nothing of them yet in person, their only interaction being via email and phone call. So far today she had only spoken to their staff, who all catered for their employers' needs and business with clockwork efficiency, and with no small amount of smouldering sexuality.

It had been the Chauffer she had encountered first, when not two hours ago the sleek black limousine had pulled up outside of Hannah's small suburban home, much to the interest of her nosy neighbours. Hannah, the twenty-six year old lady who all the locals liked because of her cheery politeness and quiet, girl-next-door demeanour was clearly being treated to something; this was a *real* limo, not the tacky kind favoured by hen parties and drunk girls in which to cruise around town on a Saturday night. They watched through twitching curtains as the slender girl walked down her garden path in a neat polka dot dress, black tights and her favourite leather boots, a mix of retro chic and punk that worked perfectly on her.

The driver got out to open her door. She was six feet tall, the very definition of statuesque beauty, short blonde hair cut close to her sharp jaw with high, elegant cheekbones. She wore an immaculate suit, black tie and a hat so-welled kept it gleamed. Her dark eyes shone as she greeted her charge.

"Miss Hannah," the woman nodded. "You look wonderful today."

With a thankyou, Hannah vanished behind mirrored glass and the driver took her seat and gunned the car out of the estate like a shark on the hunt, leaving the locals to muse what lay in store for that quiet, shy girl.

That Hannah had them all fooled was a secret joy to her.

She wrestled with nerves and anticipation as she watched the scenery whip by, further removing her from her comfort zone with every passing second. A glass of champagne already laid out for her helped a little. The car sliced its way through the suburbs and out into the countryside, following a quiet, serpentine road before turning off onto a long driveway that cut between a lengthy mass of towering trees, the evening sunlight kept out by the overhead canopy. The sense of unease that bubbled within Hannah intensified a little; she had told nobody where she was going, because who would understand or allow her to go? The fear of this venture becoming more sinister certainly worried... but the unease was outstripped by the excitement.

Finally they arrived at an ornate gate which parted for them and let them continue up the gravel driveway to arrive at the Madisons' home. It was a grand place, sitting alone amidst a grove of trees, three stories high with six separate rooms visible on the lower floor, a large oak door perfectly central atop a small stone stairwell that rose from the turning circle the car now came to rest in. The Madisons had the kind of money that most people could only dream about. This self built mansion spoke of their wealth and power.

The beautiful Chauffeur opened the door and Hannah's sturdy boots hit the gravel. She took in the majesty and style of the house as the car slid away. With tentative steps she went to the door and chimed the bell; it echoed deep within the mansion.

A breathtakingly handsome male Butler in a tailored suit answered the door; he was in his thirties, with piercing blue eyes and a manner that balanced cool subservience and control.

"Miss Hannah, it is a pleasure. The Lord and Lady of the house are thrilled that you could come."

The Butler ushered her into the massive antechamber, boots striking the polished wooden floors. A staircase ascended and split into two onto an inner balcony that led off to the upper rooms. Arched doorways on this floor led to other chambers where she could see a smattering of kitchen staff and maids setting up for evening at which Hannah was to be honoured guest. Everybody on the staff looked like a model, plucked from a glamour magazine or a catwalk and told to clean the house and prepare it for the festivities.

"Am I early?" she worried.

"Not at all. The Lord and Lady would like you to enjoy their hospitality before the evening commences. Allow me to show you to your room."

She followed him up the staircase and off into the east wing on the first floor, past framed photographs and artworks of moody landscapes and abstracts that exuded taste and style. The Butler opened the door to her bedroom, and her breath caught in her throat as she crossed the threshold.

"The finest guest bedroom," he explained. "Treat it as your own."

It was larger than the entire ground floor of her home and she fought the urge to spin on her toes with her arms outstretched. Furniture was antique and graceful atop a rich burgundy carpet. An expensive chandelier bathed the whole abode in a warm light that put her somehow at ease. There was nothing modern, no phone or television. A four-poster bed of ancient oak dominated the room, snug between two towering windows; she had never seen such a bed before, let alone slept in one, and it was all she could do not to leap up onto it and bounce with childlike abandon. A dressing table loaded with expensive beauty products waited, and the vanity mirror above reflected her marvelling expression as she took in this wonderful space.

"Your hosts request you enjoy a bath at your leisure," the handsome Butler told her, gesturing at an adjoining door she had failed to spot. "It has already been drawn for you. The Chambermaid will bring your gown for the evening and assist you if you require."

"Thank you."

His eyes showed a glimmer of warning. "Dinner is served at eight o'clock *sharp*."

Hannah understood, and allowed him to leave without another word. She languished on the bed, savouring the luxuriant silence, the calm before the inevitable storm. Everything leading up to this felt like such a blur, a dream had by someone else and viewed through a haze, a fairytale not fit for the young.

The advert she had placed online had been a whim, an act of rebellion against the mundane, wanting to experience something more than the string of weak lovers and forgettable sexual encounters the last year had provided. She was too independent for a regular lover, too easily bored, but her needs were so rarely satisfied by the men whom she allowed to speak to her in bars or take her on dates. So too were they scared sometimes by the things she wished to attempt; the men, and on occasion when curiosity prevailed, the women whom drifted in and out of her life were so often vanilla to the point of tastelessness. An advert placed in the right places on the internet was sure to unearth somebody fitting for an anonymous and deviant encounter.

Amongst the myriad of timewasters that poured in to her inbox there was a single gem, and what she had hoped for took a turn into the far more opulent and fantastical. A rich couple sought her company, charming her with honeyed words and the promise of an experience redolent of class and elegance, tailoring it to suit both their needs. In the conversations she had shared on the phone with both of them, the Lady taking the seductive lead and the Lord slicing incisively to the core of the situation, they had devised an evening that all involved would never forget.

And so now she bathed for them, cleaning away the outside world and shedding the clothes of the girl that so many foolishly thought she was. The girl she hid was to be revealed tonight, the one fuelled by lust, passion and sin. Hannah soaped her body until her skin glowed in the candlelight, scenting herself with oils that made her feel regal and exceptional. Her hands moved across bare breasts and toned thighs, sinking beneath the surface to tend to her sensitive folds. The idea of what lay ahead was enough to have prepared her already for play. A finger brushed down the crease of her sex, and her head was swimming with the idea of what delights the Madisons had laid on for her in the coming hours. She felt dizzied in the heat.

No, her sense insisted. *Don't spoil it. They want you fresh.*

She resisted her base urges and rose from the water, viewing her reflection in that cascading, infinite room; her dark hair wet against her shoulders and in thick locks across her petite, pert breasts; flat stomach and gently curving hips, shapely legs; a face that spoke of innocence but hid thoughts of depravity soon to be indulged. Her beautiful body and face were a blank canvas.

Hannah strode naked and dripping into the bedroom to find the clock on the dresser gave her a little less than an hour. She dried with a plush white towel, taking the time to tend to every inch of her skin as she rarely did when drying during the busy drudgery of real life. Then she tended to her hair, drying and styling it to bob at her dove-white shoulders. Makeup was subtle, highlighting her eyes with liner and mascara and a dark shadow, staining her lips an almost imperceptible ruby, with a hint of rouge to bring colour to her cheeks. She misted perfume across her throat and chest, basking in the sweet aroma.

As she finished, a knock sounded against the door.

She pulled the towel around her and answered to reveal a young woman in a black maid's uniform, frilled white at the neck, short sleeves and the base of her thigh-hugging skirt, clinging to her black nylons. She looked like a pinup stepped directly off the page, as beautiful as the rest of the help, red hair styled into an elaborate ponytail, face smattered with delicate freckles. The Chambermaid held a small wooden box in her hands.

"Your outfit for this evening, madam."

"Come in."

Hannah sat as the maid set the box on the dresser and popped it open. A length of white silk an inch wide lay on the lavish burgundy padding. The Chambermaid removed it, threaded it deftly through Hannah's hair and with a flourish she tied it into a fanciful bow.

"There," she said. "Perfect."

"Not quite." Hannah let the towel fall away, enjoying the change of the Chambermaid's expression; there was no awkwardness at the nudity of the guest, but a visible appreciation and a contented smile.

"Do you think the Lord and Lady of the house will like me?"

"I know they will," the Chambermaid assured her, and with professionalism cast aside, she ran her slender fingers across Hannah's upper back, tracing her spine before squeezing her shoulders. Hannah's pulse quickened. "You're wonderful."

Hannah imagined the woman bending to kiss her neck, her hands cupping her breasts and caressing nipples that hardened at the mere thought; the women she had loved before had been pretty, but none as desirable as the vintage maiden behind her.

She considered the rarity of her indulgence. It was as if she bottled up the darker girl within her, a sensual, sexual genie that she released every few months when the illusion and pressures of normalcy became too much. They were experiences to counter the view the world had of her and she loved each one; they always remained secret, because to have them was enough. Let the folks talk of Hannah the girl-next-door. It made it all the more potent when Hannah the harlot was allowed to reign. Tonight would put everything in one place, every deviant desire she had, every fantasy fulfilled in a meticulously planned evening.

"It's almost eight, are you ready?"

She took a deep, buoying breath. "I am."

The Chambermaid opened the bedroom door and allowed the Butler inside. He carried a thicker length of silk in his hands, black and opaque, and with a nod from Hannah he carefully draped it across her eyes, plunging her into darkness where every sound and smell was suddenly heightened, her arousal building with instantaneous fervour. The Butler knotted the blindfold.

The clock on the dresser chimed eight times in the anticipant stillness, and Hannah rose and felt the Butler and Chambermaid's hands grip her upper arms and guide her across the warm, tickling carpet and out of her room, naked but for the blindfold and bow.

It was time for the meal, and the menu consisted entirely of her.

2

The Chambermaid and the Butler guided her through the house, carefully down the stairwell and into the entrance of the hall; she trusted them to lead her, vision completely obstructed by the silken barrier fastened across her eyes. The house was cool, drawing gooseflesh across her skin and stiffening the dark buds of her nipples atop their perfect mounds. She wanted to see so desperately what she looked like, as naked as when she had taken her first breath but with twenty five years of growing to the womanly grandeur that was now being led like a supposedly innocent lamb to the slaughter.

There was silence throughout the house but she knew when she had entered the dining room; the carpet gave way to hardwood floors, cold beneath the soles of her bare feet, and the atmosphere shifted to a definite sense of palpable anticipation. The hush was broken by a dozen inhaled breaths from an audience she could not see watching her grand entrance. She heard her name whispered a dozen times, unable to decipher the hushed chatter that ensued from either side as her gentle captors brought her to a standstill.

A voice akin to a powerful engine growled seductively across the space, deep and affirming. "Honoured guests, may I present to you Miss Hannah."

What followed was a thunderous applause, a dozen sets of hands showing their appreciation for her exposure, her presence; she had not heard such devotion given since playing the lead in an amateur dramatics performance during her teens, and the sound and sensation brought back a heady blend of humility, narcissism and pubescent teenage hormones. She smiled, *feeling* the applause, each clap sending a gust of air against her skin. It excited her no end.

When the adulation faded she heard Mr. Madison's familiar authoritative voice again.

"We are delighted you could be here with us this evening."

She didn't reply, and the silence that followed implied an answer was expected. Her voice sounded reedy. "Thank you, sir."

The next voice was Mrs. Madison, the same she had heard over the phone but with a new quality, one of dominating strength; the Lady of the house was playing the role with zeal tonight. "Such an exquisite young thing. Doesn't she look good enough to eat?"

An approving murmur came from the crowd Hannah so desperately wanted to see.

"That's why I'm here, ma'am," she managed, barely in control of her nerves and the rising sexual kick within her. She shifted slightly to part her naked legs, allowing the cool air to caress the moistening garden she had stripped of hair that very afternoon. This brought a second wave of appreciative sounds from the gallery at either side.

The Butler and Chambermaid urged her forward and a narrow band of wood pressed against her hips: the edge of a sturdy dining table. Cooperating, she pivoted at the waist until her upper body was pressed snugly against the warm, varnished oak, stomach flat, breasts pooling against the surface. The sensation of it against her erect nipples was delightful. The crowd was silent as the help took an arm each and guided it to the adjacent edges of the table, able fingers bidding her own to clasp the wood before she felt thick leather straps looping her wrists. With a sharp tug they allowed her no give, holding her forearms to the wood with little hope of escape. Just as her hosts wanted.

What must it look like, she wondered? Hannah bent over before a waiting, unknown viewership, presented like a willing slave. She crossed her ankles to emphasise every curve of her legs, the toned calves and fatless thighs and the glorious double arch of her buttocks, pristine and waiting; the perfecting of the ripe peach on statuesque stems brought an agreeable murmur from the throng.

"Let's take off that blindfold," Mrs. Madison commanded.

The Butler's deft fingers loosened the knot and the silk was removed; the light was low enough that she did not squint, but it took her a short while to take in everything. At the head of the six-foot wooden table to which she was lashed sat two throne-like chairs where the Lord and Lady of the house sat; seeing them now in the flesh was infinitely better than the photographs she had seen thus far. Mr. Madison was an imposing figure, at least six foot five and with a physique of prime muscle and tone hidden beneath a suit she could never estimate the value of. His crystal blue eyes could have pinned her to the table as capably as the bonds at her wrists. Beside him, his wife was a vision of elegance and supremacy in a black dress that accentuated her ample bosom, slender neck exposed, hair piled into a vintage hive. Her dark eyes took in Hannah with a visible hunger.

Along each side of the table were six guests, smartly dressed, a mix of male and female, their true faces obscured by ornately designed visages, masks like those used at a masquerade. The elite wished their identities to be held secret, but all wanted to see the delights of the evening, and they were permitted to see it from all perspectives; four mirrors with six foot diagonal spans had been hauled above the table to the ceiling and secured at angles at each corner, providing guests with an unencumbered view of the beauty tethered to the wood. Finally Hannah saw herself from those vantage points, thrilled at how slender and beautiful she looked, presented like a museum's centrepiece.

The Butler and Chambermaid took up positions behind their employers and the Chauffeur appeared from the darkness to join them.

"Now," Mrs. Madison said, rising from her seat to a height of six feet, an Amazonian presence that slinked around the table, red nails gently scraping against the untarnished wood. "Let the meal begin."

The audience fell preternaturally still as the Lady of the house came behind Hannah. The younger girl released an unexpected breath as the hostess' nails etched across the flesh on either side of her spine, working a slalom between the nodes of her vertebrae all the way to her buttocks where they dug in marginally deeper, scratching the tender flesh. Lady Madison stroked her digits down the outside of Hannah's thighs and to the backs of her knees, and it took great effort to keep them from buckling at the sensuous tickling.

The Lady snapped her fingers and the Chambermaid scurried to her side carrying a small velvet stool which she placed carefully to allow her employer to sit, giving her a perfect view of Hannah's presented delicacy. Hannah gazed up at the twin mirrors in her eye line to see the tigress' eyes over the curve of her ass, just able to make out those luscious, claret red lips as they were moistened by a glistening tongue. Mrs. Madison's hands made a return journey up her inner thighs, until finally two index fingers reached the waiting, quivering lips and parted them like curtains going up on a wonderful show. Hannah could not contain a shuddering breath.

"Oh, Lady Madison..."

Mrs. Madison made a satisfied noise as she sank her lips into that pink sliver as if seeking sustenance from the limpid pool, and her action drew a satisfied smattering of applause from the gathered viewers. Hannah's gaze was held by Mr. Madison, who sat like a king surveying his queen dining on the most beautiful peasant in the land; the feeling of servitude heightened Hannah's delight as that slithering tongue worked its expert magic in her exposed, fluxing nethers. The Lady dined with skill; no extraneous noises, no clumsy motions, merely expert ministrations, lapping and licking at the engorged labia, coaxing her swollen bud to its limit and circling it in a tornado of building sensation. Hannah mewled, helpless to resist and desiring to do no such thing, but she could feel the taut knots of her knees weakening as a climax approached.

Mrs. Madison noticed the impending weakness and with a second click of her fingers The Chambermaid stepped forward with the Chauffer and kneeled dutifully beside their mistress, holding Hannah's legs at thighs and calves, forming a natural brace of perfect feminine symmetry. Mrs. Madison never broke her feast, suckling on Hannah's clitoris to evoke moans that rose in intensity.

Hannah loved it so wholly her heart ached. A dozen pairs of keen eyes peered out from impassive, pale faces, and the feeling of being scrutinized as she was brought to the heights of her pleasure made the climax crash through her with an unbridled scream. Her vision swam as a dozen masks became an ocean of millions, the sound of their rapturous applause a cacophony, a wall of sound from all angles that drowned out her cries. The Lord of the house grinned with delight.

Her senses started to return and in the mirrors above she saw Mrs. Madison, the fruits of her efforts glistening on her chin, standing and licking her fingers, preparing them for their next task. With her other hand against the small of Hannah's back and with a power against which it was futile to struggle, the Lady slid two fingers into the untended box that Hannah presented so eagerly. That tight canal was still twitching from the care given to its beautiful wrapping and Hannah felt like crying as a second orgasm started to build immediately. The twin roving digits skated across her walls, corkscrewing deeper and rolling on either side of the rough raised patch that Mrs. Madison was determined to simply tease for now, denying her the release.

Then came the contact, the Lady's fingertips brushing against her G-spot and applying such wonderful pressure as to force a raw, animalistic howl from Hannah's throat. She could no longer form a logical thought or word, gasping raggedly as the audience clapped and giggled at her efforts, but still the Lady was not done.

A third finger stretched Hannah's accommodating quim further and soon all four were roiling in and out of her, a forceful thumb teasing her clit with each twist, but Mrs. Madison had plans for that too. She brought it flush to her palm, her hand forming a shape akin to a duck's bill; the whole audience gasped, knowing what was coming, and Hannah welcomed it.

She squealed as Mrs. Madison's fingers and thumb vanished within her, lubricated with saliva and Hannah's natural tonic; she tightened only briefly in resistance, but with a flick of the Lady's wrist the hurdle of her knuckles was passed and Hannah's muscles took over, drawing the hand within her with a brief burst of exquisite pain followed by an explosion of pleasure so intense it almost blacked her out. She grunted incoherently as the Lady balled her fist within the sleeve of her sex, filling her, stretching her wide, then withdrawing, hand resuming the shape of a blade to slip out. She repeated this motion, arm pumping, the tone of her muscles defined as she worked.

With a calm tap to each of their heads, the Chambermaid and the Chauffeur responded to pre-given orders and rose to new positions; the blonde driver slid between Hannah's legs and coiled her arms around her thighs to keep her steady, tongue and lips tending to her clitoris as the lady of the house slipped her fist into the girl's sodden grove. The uniformed redhead servant perched at the edge of the table and spread Hannah's buttocks to fully expose the untouched button of her ass, and with no further urging she lowered to coat its winking collar with saliva from a deftly probing tongue.

The audience was rapt as the show came to its final climax. As her clit, ass and quim were stimulated, Hannah knew only the pleasure; shuddering orgasms more violent and fulfilling than she'd ever felt piling atop one another in a blitzkrieg of joy that fired every synapse in her brain. Logic and thought were abandoned and she relinquished herself to being used, pleasured, devoured. A final howl came as Mrs. Madison slipped her wrist, palm and fingers free of the natural glove along with a brief squirt of feminine joy, the last of which trickled down Hannah's shuddering thighs.

Warm, sweet breath rang into her left ear, bringing with it Mrs. Madison's sultry tones. "Delicious, my darling, truly wonderful."

Breathing raggedly and gasping, Hannah watched dumbly as more beautiful servants passed out glasses of champagne on steel trays and the masked harlequins drank in salute to her. Lady Madison sat back on her throne, her husband taking her hand and kissing her glistening fingers, whetting his appetite with the lingering taste of the girl chained to his table.

"Drink up," Mr. Madison instructed his guests. "The second course begins shortly."

3

Hannah wanted to sleep, so sated was she by the experience; she could have drifted off there, still pivoted over the table, as the evening went on around her. Her sex ached wonderfully and she felt it retract to a resting state, her slack muscles resuming their natural shape. The Chambermaid tended to her, ensured her hair was still perfect, the bow undisturbed, and with the help of the Chauffeur she was unbound, the straps on her wrists released. The party watched as Hannah crawled onto the table, guided by the help, unashamed. The mirrors reflected her seductive prowl and she ensured she looked into the eyes of every faceless guest, peering through their masks to show them who she was. They were hushed to silence by her fierce, animal gaze.

Mr. Madison raised a finger to halt her advance and she held her position on all fours, gazing into the mirror to see the Chauffer and the Butler at the foot of the table behind her. The woman held his hand as he stepped up onto the footstool and onto the dais. He took slow, deliberate steps towards her, each vibrating contact of his shoes against the wood making her heart rate quicken. He removed his jacket and tossed it to the Chambermaid; the fitted shirt revealed a wonderfully muscular physique and arms she would be powerless to resist. Faultless hands worked his belt and he slid it free. He came to a stop with his feet between her legs, expensive Italian shoe leather brushing against her calves.

The Madisons never looked away from her.

"Why are you here?" the Lady of the house asked.

Hannah did not falter. "To pleasure and be pleasured."

"Oh, you can do that anywhere, with anybody. A boyfriend, a random stranger found in a nightclub. Why cry out for this kind of attention?"

"Everyone thinks I'm so sweet and innocent," she explained as the Butler dropped to a kneeling position in the alcove presented by her legs. He threaded the belt underneath her and looped it through the buckle, pulling it tight until it fit snugly around her waist; he gripped it steadfastly for leverage during what was to come. "They need to know what they're missing."

"How will they ever know?" Mr. Madison said in a baritone that made her wet just to hear it.

"I'll know," Hannah said. "That's all that matters."

The Madisons smiled, satisfied, and gave the Butler a nod.

Hannah gasped as he entered her; she had been so preoccupied in conversation she had not noticed the Butler take his impressive tool from his suit paints, and now it was within her to the root, fitting snugly into her hot sanctum. She dropped her head to the table once more, raising her ass up to meet his thrusts. They were rhythmic and tender at first, but at her insistence he moved more quickly, each gliding probe met with equal commitment from her bucking hips. The slap of their thighs filled the chamber and the audience leaned forward in unabashed interest, vocalising their approval. The Butler used the belt around Hannah's waist to pull himself with both hands deeper into her hot spot. She leaned back to watch him, wrapping his tie around her wrist so they were bound together by silk and leather.

"Fuck me," she panted. His brow glistened in a sheen of sweat and the Butler quickened his pace and maintained contact with those icy-blue eyes. She was filled by his thick girth and he held it within her, allowing her own motions to bring her joy, hips roiling, squeezing his rod with muscles she barely knew she had until her peak arrived. With an unintelligible grunt she flopped against the table, shuddering like a fish plucked from the ocean. The crowd gasped and cheered.

"More," she pleaded, and eyed Mr. Madison with feral hunger, stared at his crotch. "Give me more, sir."

Mr. Madison looked to his wife, not for approval, but merely in agreement.

He stood. With measured strides he circled the table, prowling the space between audience and performers, gesturing for their activity to continue. Hannah drew on reserves of strength and bounded at the Butler, forcing his shoulders against the table. With a violent tear she ripped each button from his shirt in a single movement, bracing her fingers against the musculature of his chest as she planted her feet either side of his hips, ensuring her buttocks were hoisted high for Lady Madison to see. This was a position she adored, all her strength focused in her thighs, now glistening with sweat and hard as steel.

Mr. Madison continued his unhurried walk, never taking his eyes off her; that steely look he gave her made her sodden sex throb further and she momentarily forgot the man pinned beneath her and awaiting the lowering of that sleek crevice onto his totem. The Lord of the house had a powerful aura about him, and his whole demeanour was redolent of smooth, effortless confidence and control. It was reminiscent of a dozen older men she had desired over the years, particularly during her sexual development; her father's friends, her teachers, the businessmen she would pass in the street that never looked at her twice. They were men with manners and experience and she wanted them over any of the foolish boys that lavished her with clumsy compliments and lustful glances.

"What are you waiting for, Miss Hannah?"

"You, sir. I want you."

He stopped alongside her, reaching out to run a strong hand down the curve of her spine. The taut muscles throughout her body almost betrayed her as he caressed. He was surveying her curves like he would those of a vintage automobile, checking for imperfections and finding none. In her careful squat she held fast, so much blood coursing to her pulsing pussy that she feared passing out. The Butler smiled up at her, uncaring that she was neglecting him in favour of his boss; Mr. Madison's fingers gave her a pleasure that penetration would be unable to equal. Her eyes fluttered, teeth gritted, sweat coursing in rivulets across the tone and definition of every inch of white skin, pattering onto the table.

One hand slid over the crest of her ass and sank into the valley of her snatch, and two thick fingers brushed her outer lips, gently scissoring them between his firm digits; simultaneous his other hand dove beneath her, palm gliding over her stomach before a finger zeroed in on her clitoris.

Hannah yelped in abandon with a sudden climax so intense it starred her vision. At his mere touch her whole world went away and a spray of her feminine liquid misted the Butler's waiting cock at the same instant as her thighs gave way. Mr. Madison was there to guide her down, taking her meagre weight, spearing her gushing honeypot onto the dewed member under her. Hannah was again incapable of anything coherent, slipping him inside her and requiring Mr. Madison's strength to lift her up and down for the first few thrusts.

Attention came back just in time to see Mr. Madison shrugging off his tailored jacket and tossing it onto his throne, summoning the Chambermaid to bring the stool on which his wife had sat. He stepped up, kneeling on the table behind Hannah as she rode the Butler with rising strength.

His hands went to her cheeks and splayed, revealing the object of his affections, the tight hole that gleamed with sweat and a coating of the Chambermaid's saliva. He circled it with a finger, prodding softly to prepare it for what she so desperately craved, and in response it eased open a tiny, tantalising fraction.

"Do it, Mr. Madison," she pleaded. "Take me. Own me."

He licked a finger and sank it into the tight collar of her anus and she gasped as both holes were tended to; anal sex was a rarity for her but she loved it, the sensation so powerful and intrusive it made her giddy now as the moment encroached. Her rear canal drew his finger deeper, lubed with spit and sweat, until he was within to the knuckle, brushing her walls, flexing that finger to widen her for him.

"Fuck me," she begged. "Both of you, fuck me together."

In the mirrors above, Mr. Madison's cock emerged from his pinstripe trousers, a baton of meat almost nine inches long, a wand devoted to the giving of pleasure. Mr. Madison's left hand went to her hair, taking a handful to steel himself; his right gripped the belt still taut around her waist. Guiding her like a willing puppet he brought her eager hole to the head of his weapon. Her asshole blossomed slowly but surely until it enveloped that bulbous bell; a strident yap escaped her lips but she held fast, easing backwards, inch by splendid inch, filling her to the brim, each new centimetre fading from discomfort to joy until he was in her all the way.

He eased her closer by the hair and her bridle, her back arching, the meat inside her bending, attuned to her motion. His smiling mouth peppered her neck and throat with flimsy kisses, and his hot breath resonated in her ear: "Good girl..."

She had to drop to her knees astride the Butler, unable to hold herself up as twin rods infiltrated her intimate spaces, packing her tightly. Nerves were alive, dense pockets of fibre massaged by two glorious dicks, reaming her wider with slow, confident thrusts. At first they moved in opposite directions but soon synchronised, penile pistons plunging into her, intensity building. The audience and the Lady of the house were spellbound at what transpired before them, three beings locked into one beautifully deviant act.

Hannah looked into the eyes of the Butler; as handsome as he was, they were not the eyes that made her whole soul boil. "Turn me over,"

She gasped as Mr. Madison's dick slipped out of her, the tiny gape of her bottom closing but ready for more. With four powerful hands they flipped her as if she weighed nothing and she braced her feet to allow the Butler's access to her porthole. In he went with ease, a smaller but no less intense presence than the Lord of the house, who held her knees firmly as he brushed the head of his length against the swollen folds of her lips.

"Put it inside," Hannah begged. "I need it. Fuck me, Mr. Madison."

Never looking away from her, he gave her what she wanted, slipping into her lustrous pink canal like the final piece of a jigsaw puzzle, gliding in with measured pumps of his hips. He stroked her inner thighs and then took her by the crook of her knees until she had no control over her stance; she was theirs now, the plaything of the servant and the master of the domain. The former reached around and caressed her breasts, tugging at her nipples.

Madison's eyes were on her, lovingly, boring through her soul and seeing the truth of her; they elated as much as the act in which they were inexorably locked. She was about to come again, every muscle below her waist squeezing hard enough to compact coal into diamond. It was enough to finish the Butler off and the impression of his voluminous gift flooding into her kicked her over the edge. She flew on the wings of her climax, soaring high above the room, each mirror a distant screen displaying the reality, but her mind was momentarily beyond that body, floating for a stretch of blissful seconds, before crashing down in a shuddering, hollering, gasping finish.

With tenderness unrivalled the master and Butler kissed the flesh of her neck, shoulders and cheeks, then slid from her to leave her trembling and exposed at the centre of an adoring, applauding audience.

"Bravo," Lady Madison cheered. "Bravo, my dear."

Hannah drew her legs up to herself as the more vibrant memories of her sexual history drifted through the miasma of post-coital reminiscence: losing her virginity in her parents' bed to a college friend; a drunken back-alley fumble with a girl at University; video-calling a boyfriend and masturbating for him while he returned the favour. These were her experiences and because she had kept them quiet everybody assumed she was incapable of such sexual abandon. Tonight was the pinnacle, her desire unbridled. The sheep's clothing had fallen away; the wolf was here to stay.

The Butler had withdrawn to the shadows and Hannah was alone on the table as the murmuring of the crowd died away. She unfolded languidly, stretching like a satisfied lioness, a broadening smile on her flushed face as she watched her reflected self from four angles, sprawling and naked but for the still-perfect bow in her hair.

"I want dessert," she purred.

4

The Chauffeur and the Chambermaid strode forward from either side, heels clicking in unison against the hardwood floor, and they took Hannah by the upper arms and dragged her to the edge of the table before the Madisons; the Lord's rod still protruded hugely from his suit trousers, his wife now standing beside him, proudly massaging it to keep it primed for its final task.

Hannah angled her head back, hanging off the edge of the desk, viewing her benefactors upside down just as desired. Lady Madison stroked her chin and throat gently as if tenderising it, slackening it for the finale.

"Such a beautiful girl, certainly not the innocent little creature many would believe. Prove it, once and for all. Open up."

With a deep breath Hannah extended her jaw as far as she could and within a heartbeat the lady threaded her husband's cock into the waiting, wet maw, diving deeper with each careful thrust until she had taken it all. The crowd gasped and applauded her efforts; with each shove they watched her throat distend to accommodate Mr. Madison's lance. Each withdrawal brought with it ropes of saliva, but she did not gag, not once. The two female helpers flanked Hannah and held her arms in place, flat to the wood so she could not resist. Not that she wanted to; this was her denouement, the rush to the final curtain.

Hannah took him with aplomb, loving the sensation; her desire to have her mouth reamed like this had developed over years of giving evermore perfect oral sex to boyfriends; she had honed her gag reflex down to virtual zero, and wanted nothing more than to be throatfucked by a cock that would take her to any limits she may still possess.

Then he caught her just right, his hot cock brushing her uvula, constricting her throat and she choked temporarily. Mr. Madison withdrew his sword from her saliva-slick scabbard and she gasped for air, eyes prickling with tears.

"Magnificent!" Mrs. Madison complimented. "Just wonderful, I've never seen skills like it."

She took him again, rocking her head against his cock as his hips gave liquid, perfect strokes and his wife looked on in awe. This was it, the icing on her perfect cake, where she was nothing more than a fuck hole. The sheer thought of it made her as wet now as she had been throughout the encounter and she wanted desperately to touch her crimson clit to release the building tension, but her hands were pinned tight. It burned down below and she yearned for release as much as she yearned for air; Madison held his cock so deep within her mouth he starved her lungs of what she needed.

She could not breathe, suspended in this infinite moment, riding the wave that would result in a blackout. Shadows crept at the edge of her vision.

Like a guardian angel, Mrs. Madison swept in to trigger a chain reaction ending in her release, running her hands across Hannah's body, circling the dark buds of her nipples, dancing across her toned abdomen and skating the den of her sex before hitting their target perfectly. With a stifled groan Hannah came with an unmatched intensity. The shadows were joined by spots speckling her vision. Spurred to his goal by the final tightening of Hannah's throat, Mr.

Madison held back no longer, testicles rising against his body as they launched their contents into the willing well in which he was immersed.

She gulped down the saline as he unsheathed from her for the last time, sucking down oxygen along with it, vision whiting out. She breathed as if coming up from a dark ocean. The crowd clapped in awe.

Hannah rose up onto her side, hands splayed and supporting her weight as her entire body shivered. She was fully exposed now and primal, animalistic, her mascara streaming like black tears, her breath coming in harsh, ragged gusts.

She ripped the bow from her hair and discarded it without a second thought.

"Take off your masks," she rasped. "You've seen the real me. Now show me yourselves."

The faceless masks fell to reveal the genuine faces behind, twelve sets of flushed and familiar features; the first boyfriend who had called her frigid at fourteen when she had not been ready to lose herself to him; the girls who had taken his whispers and spread hurtful lies and crafted the identity of innocence which she had started to believe; lovers she had taken when she had cast off the shackles of inadequacy and shyness who had been scared by her ferocity. Through her planning with the Madisons, all had been invited, accepted, masked and made to watch; it spoke of the hidden desires of each one of them that not a single soul had refused. Those who thought she was innocent now knew better; those who had not wished to indulge her in her desires now knew what they had missed out on.

She slithered from the table with a new confidence in her gait. Mr. and Mrs. Madison humbly stepped aside as she sat in one of the decorative thrones, draping her bare legs across the seat of the other, filling them both as if she was the true queen of the house. The guests were ushered out silently, faces from her past vanishing into the night. She wondered how many of them would try to make renewed contact with her, and could not decide yet if she would pander to them.

She realised how hungry she was, and before she could speak the Chambermaid appeared with a black silk robe which she slipped into, and the Butler arrived with a silver tray with a domed serving dish from beneath which the most delicious smells escaped. They laid the table for three, and Hannah and the Madisons prepared to dine together, but for Hannah, sexual appetite sated, the real banquet had already ended.

She knew deep within her satisfied bones that it would not be her last.

POWER
A Poem

Surrender your soul and offer it up
As a fragile spark I will kindle to fire.
I have no whims, only the will,
To make you burn as bright as a star.

Throw yourself at my mercy,
I have it in spades, to care and caress.
I'll dig deep within you, nurture your heart until
It grows and swells for me alone.

Call me 'sir', but it's not a demand.
A choice, a desire, a sign of control.
But mine is mere illusion, for
It is you who is forever in charge.

The submission is yours to give.
My relentless desire is yours to take.
And though you lay at my feet,
The power lies with you.

SUBMISSIVE DESIRE

1

Veronica strode on perfectly shapely legs across the bedroom towards the desk, leaning closer to the webcam so that in the software playback window she loomed large, intimidating and severe, dark red lips spitting every word:

"What did I say about touching?"

In the larger display window on her monitor, the man dropped his hands back to his side, away from the mighty erection that he was so desperate to tend. Mr. Friday Night was sitting in his computer chair, trousers tugged down to his thighs, restricting his leg movement. Earlier during the session he had stretched a ring of taut rubber down his shaft and around the base of his scrotum, heightening pleasure and ensuring he stayed engorged and on the edge of exquisite release.

"You're desperate to touch it, aren't you?" she mused, her clipped English accent like delicious poison to the client's ears; she was in the room with him yet he was countless miles away, and he was a total slave to her bidding, just as he had requested.

"Yes, Miss Veronica," he said.

"I was showing off my outfit and you couldn't resist breaking the rules and sneaking a quick stroke, could you?"

"Sorry Mistress, it won't happen again."

Even with the average quality of his webcam she could see the sweat beading on his forehead, and see the tension in his sturdy jaw. Mr. Friday Night – a suitable enough moniker, for that was the time their sessions together always took place – was amongst the most handsome of her regular clients, well built, well dressed and well spoken, ever the gentleman when discussing his desires and furnishing payment, and ever the willing slave when he threw control over to her. This, their fifth session in as many weeks, was as smooth and enjoyable as she could ever hope for. To Mr. Friday Night her character was set now, a dominating presence that forbade him from enjoying himself until she told him to. Though the scenario and costume may change and different kinks were explored, it was always very much the same: she dressed for him, humiliated him, and he relished in the joy of being verbally abused and ordered to obey. From his physical prowess and wardrobe – for he often wore a smart suit during their cam-time – she assumed he was a high-powered executive somewhere, the master of his own little world, accustomed to getting his own way. His underlying desires, however, the fantasies he so desperately wanted made reality, were so far the opposite way that he could likely not disclose them in his everyday world and day-to-day life. Veronica wondered if he was married, or in a relationship that wasn't able to provide him with fulfillment for his submissive side. That was not her business: what *was* her concern was making sure he got his money's worth, and she prided herself on being the best at what she did.

"Now where were we?" she pondered, then retreated from the camera, revealing herself once more, keeping her back to him as she walked, knowing he would not dare touch himself again. Mr. Friday Night would see her flawlessly round buttocks, wrapped in a tight red leather skirt – which he had bought for her and had shipped out in time for their session tonight – slinking away atop her shapely legs. Calves and thighs were taut within black fishnet holdups that traced a hypnotic criss-cross down to six inch red heels that accentuated every muscle in her heavenly pins. Above her slender waist she wore a black silk blouse that gave off a sensual sheen in the lamplight of her spotless bedroom. Her fingers and forearms were wrapped up to the elbow in red leather gloves, similarly purchased by Mr. Friday Night; the thick material creaked as she flexed her fingers around the handle of the riding crop she brandished. Her outfit alternated red and black like a devilish checkerboard. Tracing the curve of her spine was her strawberry blonde hair, coiled into a sinuous, perfect plat. Her eyes glimmered from behind black-framed designer spectacles.

"Thank you for spoiling your Mistress," she purred, gently tapping the tip of the crop against her calves. She raised one leg to the bed and pivoted, thrusting the faultless peach of her bottom out so the lower curve of her cheeks emerged from beneath the leather skirt, soft white flesh visible between the garment and the ornate band of the holdups. A gloved hand squeezed the flesh, came down hard with a stinging slap that made her shiver with personal delight, and an echo of her own desires spread deep within her and was swiftly pushed away.

"You wish you were here, don't you? Spread before me so I can *discipline* you." On the word 'discipline' she whipped the crop through the air, making a scintillating *whoosh* sound. "I do one-to-one sessions for only my favourite clients. I can't decide if you would be one of the lucky few..."

A look to the screen showed Mr. Friday turning his face skyward as if in prayer to the heavens, begging for release. "It sounds wonderful, Miss Veronica. But..."

She turned to him. "But?" As if in warning, she lightly rapped the leather tag at the end of the whip into her palm.

"I don't think my wife would approve."

Her suspicions confirmed, it didn't change her opinion of him in the slightest; his money was good and she relied on the baser desires of men – and indeed women – to fund her chosen line of work. She merely felt a distant pang of disappointment that she'd never be able to tend to his fantasies in person. He was handsome, and to tie him to the bed and lash him senseless would be a joy as much to her as it would be to him.

Her act held and she arched an eyebrow. "And would she really approve if she knew what you were doing right now?"

"Probably not," he laughed nervously.

She rarely rose her voice or played at losing her temper, unless it was what they asked for, but she had perfected a tone of measured disdain over countless cam sessions and real-life scenarios. She employed it now.

"You pathetic worm, your tastes are so appalling your wife won't even indulge them. You come crawling to me for gratification." She lashed the crop against the edge of her desk so hard it made Friday jump, cock bobbing, strained within its ring and seeping a distinct trickle of fluid from its swollen head.

She had a profile of him in her head and knew from previous

sessions what he liked, how he enjoyed being talked down to, and she incorporated this new knowledge into her ever-changing script. "Playing happy families but as soon as her back's turned, here you are. I bet you can't even satisfy her, that's why you're here with me and she's out somewhere screwing around with a real man."

"Yes Miss Veronica, I'm your pathetic little maggot."

She placed one heel against the edge of the desk, skirt hiking up past her thighs to reveal her pussy, fully exposed to the air without panties. Her shaven cleft glistened with moisture, ready for attention. She pushed the crop against it, angling it sideways to allow its fine edge to descend a few millimetres into the furrow.

"This is just another pussy you'll never make your own. Never satisfy."

Veronica licked her own musky residue from the leather, shivering in delight. With her leg raised and body framed on camera from head to knee, she sank her gloved hand to her eager garden and spread her labia with a slow, teasing motion, playing the leather-padded buds of her fingertips through the shallow moisture.

This is what Friday liked most of all; watching her play and bring herself to orgasm while he was powerless to do anything, then joining her in the final moments of climax.

She moaned suggestively. "Oh, that's incredible. Look at how wet I've made myself. You'd never be able to get me in this state, would you?"

"No, Mistress Veronica," came the distant punter's reply. She brought the crop down across the desk again. Her attention honed onto her clitoris, working around it in tightening circles before grazing its fleshy dome. The roughness of the leather brought extra sensation and she fought to keep her knees sturdy in the face of encroaching pleasure. The nipples of her petite breasts were hard against the silk blouse, visible as distinct points through the fine material.

Her voice quavered. "Are you ready, you deviant little perv?"

"I am, Miss Veronica, I need to come," he said.

"Beg me," she demanded. *Whoosh-crack!* A further whip of the crop. "Beg me!"

"Please let me come, Miss, I'm begging you."

She waited until she was cresting her own orgasm. The dam of sensation was ready to burst, founts of joy already arcing through her.

The rising power came to a head. "Come. Come now; shoot your hot load for me."

She saw him reach for his rod, and even the slightest of touches was all it took; seed spilled in a thick trickle across his cock and splashed his thighs. As always when she reached climax on cam, she was only half able to pay attention; the mind of the character she played was with Mr. Friday, but her true self was off to play in her own memories and fantasies and ideal scenarios. She rolled through beds long-since tumbled in with men whose gifts she had tasted and whose prowess she had been floored by; she straddled faces and was pushed against nightclub walls; wrestled into submission in the back of a police car and spanked by her favourite teacher; she was collared, cuffed and made to do the bidding of a dominant soul who was intent to violate her most vulnerable of areas. What was reality and what was fiction didn't matter here. It was inseparable, all fodder for her pleasure.

With the sensations subsiding she came fully back to the present. On screen Mr. Friday panted, sated, trying to hide the self-conscious demeanour of a man who had just climaxed for an audience he couldn't really see and didn't really know.

"Thank you, Miss Veronica," he managed. "Wonderful as ever."

She flexed the riding crop between both hands and became Miss Veronica once more. "You're welcome, Mr. Friday. Same time next week?"

"You can count on it."

Then the call was ended from his side and she closed down the vid-chat software. With her orgasm fading, she sat on the edge of the bed and took off the heels, peeled off the gloves and tucked them away into a drawer filled with costumes, toys and other paraphernalia used during her cam sessions. It had almost become a ritual, packing away the items of her work like tidying her desk, and it was mental as well as physical; the Miss Veronica persona retreated into another part of her mind, ever prepared to return when needed.

A quick check of her phone showed that Phoebe had text to say she was running a little late, but they were still to meet in the usual place. That was typically Phoebe, never quite in charge of what was going on around her.

Even with Phoebe's delay, Veronica wouldn't have enough time to shower before their meeting, so opted to leave on the fishnets and the silk blouse, replacing the leather skirt with a knee-length denim number and slipping on a pair of her favourite boots. She swiftly removed the blood-red lipstick Mr. Friday always insisted on and applied some subtle lip stain, misted a final spray of perfume, grabbed her handbag and jacket and was out the door and on the street before she realised she hadn't put on panties.

The last vestige of Miss Veronica whispered: *Oh well, I've done worse* and gave her cause to giggle.

2

Milligan's was always their first and often only port of call on a Friday; it was secluded and refined enough in its tastes that the clubbing crowd cleared out early in search of louder watering holes with far lower standards, leaving it to those who enjoyed a conversation with their drink. Slipping into their usual booth with their usual bottle of white wine between them, Phoebe was still giggling at the account of what Veronica had been up to not ten minutes prior to their meet.

"And he actually sits there on his hands like he's told, like an obedient little puppy?" Phoebe's glass was up to her lips when Veronica responded.

"An obedient little puppy with a raging hard on, yeah."

With an adorable snort, Phoebe's wine splashed up onto her narrow nose, which she quickly swept dry, ensuring her shoulder length blonde hair had not been similarly speckled. She let this round of laughter escape and looked at her friend over the rim of her glass.

"You're a wild one. So then you just – what? Fingered yourself silly while he watched?"

"It's your gift with language that really endears you to me," Veronica laughed. "In a nutshell, yeah. That's what he asked for, and he bought me a few things to go with it. Some clients are really vague, some are really specific. Some just like to be told off, to be humiliated. I even have guys who just call to chat about their week, the weather, whatever."

"I don't know what's worse," Phoebe pondered. "Asking to be called a pathetic little prick, or being such a pathetic little prick you just talk about what you watched on TV last night!"

Veronica giggled. "To each his own. I don't judge, certainly not when they're paying me."

Phoebe was the only close friend who knew about Veronica's way of paying the rent. It was not intentionally a secret; she was open enough if people asked, but it wasn't the lead-in topic to a conversation with a stranger. Phoebe took it all in her stride; they had met through mutual acquaintances over a year ago and had become fast friends, as much due to Phoebe's openness and acceptance when it came to sexuality as due to their mutual hobbies and positive outlooks. Veronica found talking to Phoebe about her exploits kept her grounded; with much of the week spent playing different characters or versions of herself for the benefit of others, it was always nice to remember who she was, that what she did was a job. Her uniform was more likely to be a corset rather than a shirt embroidered with a company logo, but both were means to a living. These Friday nights were a refuge where she could be herself, discuss what she wished with a friend eager to hear, laugh about the absurdity of it and unburden herself of her worries.

"So how are things with Mark?" Veronica ventured, and was met with a roll of the eyes.

"I'm here with you on a Friday night," Phoebe said by way of explanation. "Now don't get me wrong, this is my best night of the week, but tonight should be ending with me biting the pillow while my boyfriend rails me into oblivion, don't you think?" Now it was Veronica's turn to snort into her wine and spray a fine mist of alcohol across her beautifully pale skin. "No, he's off with his friends, watching their movies and drinking their beer in their little gang. They've all got girlfriends sitting at home unfulfilled, you know!"

The first glass of wine was almost gone and, as expected, had rushed straight to Phoebe's head. She was not slurring whatsoever but her tongue was more relaxed, the words and feelings spilling out in a giddy torrent. Veronica was in stitches. Phoebe was one of the most relentlessly verbose people Veronica had ever met, and with the slightest hint of alcohol and a relaxed atmosphere Phoebe always let go, the floodgates opening, her words coming out in a stream-of-consciousness delivery punctuated by big expressions and bigger hand movements.

She ploughed on. "He assumes he's doing me a favour – and he is, by the way, because I love you – by gallivanting off with his precious little butt-buddies. I know we're supposed to be all aloof and cool and pretend we're not as dirty-minded as guys, but I could go home tonight, throw on the sluttiest lingerie known to humanity – and trust me, I've got it, and I've done it before – spread myself wide for him coming home, and he'd either hop on, do his thing in two minutes or just flop down next to me snoring before I can even say 'Fuck me, stud, fuck me!"

Veronica blinked back tears of laughter as Phoebe took in a long breath to steady herself. In the booth across from them, a couple – whether part of a long relationship or on a first date – were looking their way, unable to tune out Phoebe's rant.

"Sorry," she said, cheeks flushing. The couple shared a gaze in silence, and then the woman gave a shrug and a wrinkle of her nose as if an agreement with the sentiment she'd heard. The man looked embarrassed, then bolstered. He drained his glass and led his lady by the hand to the door.

"See, everyone's at it but me!" Phoebe said. "I'm bitching, I know. I just wish he'd do as he's told, sometimes. Learn to appreciate what he's got, to know that sometimes I want to be romanced, wined and dined, made love to...and sometimes I *do* just want to be fucked like there's no tomorrow. I'm not all 'woman-in-charge' all the time, but he needs to be whipped into shape."

"Well, I do have a riding crop, if you want to borrow it," Veronica teased.

Phoebe laughed, drained her glass and refilled it from the bottle, and the whole time Veronica saw the cogs ticking behind her big brown eyes, until finally those eyes sparked with an idea and her mouth formed the earliest hints of a deviant smile.

"Do you still do the one-on-one sessions?"

"Yes," Veronica said slowly. "Why?"

"You know what I'd really like?"

"What's that?" Veronica said, draining her own glass and filling it back to the brim, knowing where Phoebe's mind was venturing.

"Would you consider it?"

"You haven't actually said anything yet," Veronica reminded her.

"You know what I'm going to say, don't you?"

"I have an inkling."

"So would you consider it?"

Veronica liked playfully antagonising Phoebe and she kept presenting the perfect opportunity. "Consider what?"

"You're a cocktease, you know that?" Phoebe grinned.

"Professionally."

Phoebe leaned in conspiratorially, voice lowered to a whisper, though there was now nobody in the vicinity who would hear them.

"How about taking Mark under your wing for an hour or so?"

Veronica held her friend's gaze and maintained her smile, but alarm bells rang before the sentence was even out of Phoebe's mouth. That was the kind of indecent proposal that started out as fun and full of excitement and resulted in broken hearts and friendships.

"You've had one too many wines already," she laughed.

"No, I'm serious. I can crack the whip all I like but it's no substitute for an *actual* whip!"

"And what would I do?" Veronica asked, curious but not for a second seriously entertaining the notion.

"Whatever it is you do," Phoebe said excitedly. "Humiliate him, strip him down, throttle him, give him some of that cat-o-nine-tails action. Make sure he learns that he should appreciate what he's got, learn some respect."

"Why don't we just go the whole hog and give him a good pegging?" Veronica joked, instantly regretting it when she saw the sparkle in Phoebe's eyes become a supernova.

"Yes!" she beamed.

"Phoebe, I was joking, it's not happening."

Phoebe slumped back in her chair and gave a mock pout. "Oh, why not?"

"Oh, I don't know, for starters he's my best friend's boyfriend, I rather think that makes it a little risky when it comes to being able to look each other in the eye afterwards. It'll cause trouble, trust me."

"If I promised you it wouldn't?"

"That's easy to say but it'll change something between us. It's like where you date a friend's ex. They say they're fine with it, but even if they hated the guy when they split, he was still theirs for long enough that they'll hate you for it."

Phoebe leaned forward, the spark still glimmering but now from behind a sheen of melancholy. "What if I told you he was soon to *be* an ex?"

"What?" Veronica said, lecturing tone evaporating as she leaned forward to take Phoebe's hands.

"Oh, don't get all soppy," Phoebe insisted. "I'm fine. My peace with it has long been made. The spark hasn't been there since after that first night, and you know it." She wasn't upset, just calm and resigned, and Veronica could tell this was the first time she had spoken her intentions out loud. Phoebe's whole posture changed throughout, to strengthen, and to puff up with confidence. "I knew there wouldn't be wedding bells a while ago, but I think I just pushed it away because he's *nice*. He's reliable, and he's sweet, and it's easy to forget your world isn't on fire when your world's *comfortable*."

Veronica squeezed her hand tighter and gave a reassuring smile. The wicked glint in Phoebe's eyes gradually returned. "And what better way to send him off into the world than with a goodbye gift to soften the blow and prepare him for the next lucky lady."

"Man him up by turning him into a little bitch?" Veronica posited, and felt a mix of unease tempered with potential thrill ripple through her as she realised she was now entertaining the idea.

"Exactly," Phoebe said. "Plus, I get to see you on the job."

Veronica cocked her head. "You didn't say anything about you being there!"

"Maybe not there in the room," she agreed, "But I've got a webcam gathering dust and I'd hate to miss out on a front row seat."

Veronica let the thought roll around for a while, unable to stop a surprised and willing smile creep across her features. She divided the last of the wine between their glasses.

"Drink up, lady," she said. "We've a plan to hatch."

*

In an act of celebrating an impending change, the girls fled from *Milligan's* before a second bottle of wine and found themselves in a much rowdier bar, sipping cocktails with vaguely pornographic names. They found a freestanding table in a corner and conducted their conversation at a raised volume in order to hear each other over the floor-shaking bass. The attention of gentlemen, and those with far less gentlemanly intentions, was deferred for the time being. With fruity alcohol consumed in great quantities their tongues loosened further; pertinent points were recorded as notes on Phoebe's smartphone to be arranged into a more achievable plan during the daylight hours.

Certain things were said between them that were assumed forgotten, revelations thought lost amidst the din of revelry, but Phoebe wasn't so intoxicated that she forget to jot them down on her phone, and a digital memory chip remembers everything.

3

Veronica awoke on Saturday morning with only the vaguest suggestion of a hangover, and following a hot shower and breakfast she was alert and ready for the day. The earliest hours of her night out were fresh in her memory, and even without alcohol she was still willing and eager to indulge in Phoebe's plan. She liked Mark but did not consider him a friend, and as long as he accepted their proposal and the breakup with Phoebe, she would be more than happy to help send him on his way.

Would he say yes? The majority of her clients were men with submissive desires, and though not universal she had learned that most men harboured some form of clandestine desire to be dominated, to have a woman take total control. Whether that involved merely letting her have total say of what was done, or extended to humiliation, spanking or even anal play was more changeable.

The latter portion of the their evening blended together in a haze of thrumming bass line, sweat and booze; she recalled snatches of conversations with Phoebe and a parade of men asking for her number, all of whom she had politely declined for the simple reason of finding them unattractive or uninteresting. Waking up alone was a relief; she had not made a stupid mistake and succumbed to a desperate one night stand. A fragment of last night's lost chatter tumbled back into her brain; telling Phoebe that sometimes she felt lonely, that despite her sexual exploits she was never having her own needs serviced by someone she liked. This made her cringe a little, but that she had said it to Phoebe was far better than spilling it to a stranger, let alone a male who would have used it as a cloying attempt to bed her under the pretence of selfless chivalry.

Phoebe had vowed to have the conversation with Mark today, and to do it in the right order; first to break up with him, so he knew it was final, then offer the 'farewell package.' It was patently ludicrous when she examined it like that, and certain to fail. Veronica wondered if Mark, no doubt crushed by the news of becoming single, would even entertain the idea of not only being traded as a commodity by his former girlfriend and her best friend, but the trade being done with the express purpose of having him humiliated and *trained*.

It was a stupid idea. The cold light of day brought the absurdity of it all into sharp focus; what sounded fun, daring and definite under pub lighting and the blanket of alcohol was now a ridiculous dead end while cooler, sober heads prevailed. Mark would be crushed, and they had zero right to do this to him.

She reached for her phone to call Phoebe to halt the second part of their plan; the breakup was going ahead but there was no way they'd humiliate the man further by suggesting he was an inconsiderate lover who needed to be taught a few things.

Before she could dial, her phone chirped with a message coming the other way from her friend. Were it not tempered by the ubiquitous smiley face icon, it would have been austere in its simplicity:

It's over. He's in.

*

With her illusions shattered of just how much nobility a man could muster when faced with the promise of any form of sexual encounter, Veronica took herself off shopping to while away Saturday afternoon. Between the buying of two pairs of shoes, a summer dress and a retro 70s lamp for her flat, she conversed with Phoebe over the phone.

The call was a summation of what had happened when Phoebe had announced to Mark she desired for them to split.

"I just told him it wasn't working out, there was no spark there," Phoebe explained.

"And he wasn't upset?"

"How upset can you be after nine weeks and just about as many fucks?"

"You've such a way with words, Phoebe, it staggers me," Veronica giggled as she wandered the aisles of the department store, stopping every few feet to examine a new pair of heels.

"He didn't seem too bothered. I told you, we're not talking the romance of a lifetime here. We're a brief and sometimes pleasant diversion in each other's lives."

"So did you tell him that he's hardly a sexual firecracker?"

"Not in so many words," Phoebe conceded. "But I did say that you've had your eyes on him for a while and wanted to make a man of him..."

Veronica nearly dropped a pair of killer red heels. "You put it all on me?"

"He bought it!" Phoebe laughed. "He jumped at the offer surprisingly quickly. Apparently he's been a fan of yours since the night he found out what you did. He's even bought a few of the clips you've put online. *Including* the pegging one."

"No way!" That was loud enough to draw the attention of another shopper. She was glad she hadn't blurted out something more explicit, and hurried to an adjacent aisle as her cheeks flushed.

"I swear!"

"The dirty little sod," Veronica said quietly, ensuring she didn't draw an audience. The online store she had set up gave a tally of every anonymous purchase made, and to know that some of them had been Mark was unusually stirring. "So he knows what's in store for him. Now that you know he's kinkier than you imagined, does that change anything?"

Phoebe laughed away the question. "I wanted a sexual dynamo, not a dirty deviant. Anyway, how are you fixed for tonight?"

Veronica couldn't believe this had gone from alcohol-assisted girl-talk into a fully-fledged fantasy in less than a day. Nobody had booked a session with her this evening, digitally or in the flesh, so her night would be spent on a live cam trawling for business, teasing and tempting the horny and lonely into handing over their cash. Tonight was as good a night as any. Nerves and excitement wrestled for position within her.

"Let's do it."

She heard Phoebe squeal with exaggerated delight and clap her hands. "I'll let him know."

"No. *I'll* let him know," Veronica said, shifting her tone to one of stern domination. Phoebe made a satisfied 'ooh' sound and laughed with elation.

"I'll text you his number."

"Good. And you're absolutely sure you want to see all this on cam?"

"Darling, I wouldn't miss this for the fucking world."

They said their goodbyes and ended the call, and within seconds a message came through that contained Mark's phone number. She thought of waiting, but the taste of anticipation was far too rich, so she ensured she swept off to a corner of the store and checked there was nobody around to hear before dialing.

Mark picked up with a confused, "'Hello?" because Veronica knew his phone would have displayed an unknown number.

She slipped effortlessly back into her performance; Miss Veronica came from within, a second identity that was very much her but separate somehow, taking over when the time was right. "Hello, Mark," she spat quietly.

The silence on the other end of the line worried her for a brief second, but Mark soon worked out what was afoot. His tone changed to a lascivious drawl. "Hello Mistress…"

"Wipe that smirk of your face you pathetic little prick," she barked. "You think I'm here to be your plaything? You think you can leer at me like that?"

"Um, no Miss Veronica, I was just – "

"Shut up, I don't want to hear another word from you, do you understand?" The silence on the line suggested he had quickly readjusted to the rules. "Good. I expect you on my doorstep at precisely 7pm tonight. Not a second before or a second later. Is that clear?"

He remained silent, adhering to the rules with admirable accuracy.

"Good boy." She gave him the address. "Oh, and should it all get too much for you…" Regardless of what was to happen, she still had a professional duty and it was not worth the risk to flout the rules, even for a friend. "The safeword is 'foxtrot'. That should be easy for a worthless clown like you to remember. Now I want to hear that you understand."

His voice had a faltering quality to it now, as if realising that his perceptions and the reality of the evening might not entirely match up. "I understand, Miss Veronica, I understand."

She hung up without another word. She allowed her domineering persona to retreat, so she was merely Veronica when she spotted the face of a middle-aged woman peer from behind a rack of shoes. She had missed the lady entirely when checking she was alone. The woman's face was flushed tomato red, wide-eyed, and Veronica felt so embarrassed until she noticed the woman's smile.

"You'll have to teach me a few things, my love; I've wanted to do that with my husband for years..."

*

With the arrangement made, and a willing-to-learn forty something given a few handy tips to introduce her husband to the world of submission, Veronica left the department store and made for the local adult emporium, a place that had become a one stop shop when buying kit for her line of work. The sign above the door declared it as *Pulse*. It was swept away from the main high streets, sitting between a betting shop and dressmakers, and had a simple window display with three mannequins dressed in lingerie and vibrant wigs. Nothing there caught her eye; the store always put its more traditional items in the window to lure in pedestrians, but they would soon have their eyes opened upon stepping inside.

Expectations would have one assume it would be dingy and populated by less than sound characters, but *Pulse* had not become the best reputed adult store in the region and beyond by having poor standards. It was brightly lit with hardwood floors underfoot; every step taken within made a noise, forcing patrons to be empowered by their presence there. Sex was not something to be embarrassed by and the design of the store supported that truth. Upbeat music played across the sound system, but it was just as likely to be playing classical to mirror the eclectic tastes and styles of the staff that worked there. Veronica loved the place; she was a regular customer and everybody on payroll knew her, and upon entering she wondered who would be working today. She had friendships with some, and more professional relationships with others, which in turn meant she had seen them at their most exposed. The cash register was currently unoccupied.

Merchandise was neatly ordered into aisles, ranging from the kind of lingerie displayed in the window to the more specialist material; the deeper one ventured into the store, the more explicit and fetish-centric the goods became. Mannequins at the back wore full-body black vinyl suits and fetish wear, and racks of sex toys that were more than intimidating to the idle punter were poised in glass cases waiting to be taken home. A sex swing hung from the ceiling, and a moulded rubber penis strapped to a vibrating saddle sat on a raised plinth, an alluring tease for the wealthiest customers. There were two other patrons in the shop, and it always tickled her to see the diverse mix; a man in a finely tailored suit browsing the adult DVDs, and a woman who exuded refined manners examining a ball gag. This was a far cry from the dirty-old-man brigade, and the place was so much better for it.

Veronica headed past the flimsy lace lingerie, following the scent of latex that was rich down one aisle, finding herself in a fetishist's playground of gleaming rubber and plastic. She wanted to be fresh and new for her encounter with Mark tonight; nothing already worn, nothing used. He should consider himself lucky.

From the stock room emerged the on duty staff-member, and Veronica smiled as she saw the feminine eyes brighten as they fixed on hers. Maisy was an alternative goddess; the punk attitude made flesh, painted and pierced accordingly. She was a petite and slender girl with shoulder length blood-red hair and more tattoos than Veronica had ever seen on a person; multicoloured ink covered her forearms and biceps. The vest she wore accentuated her perky breasts and displayed the artwork on her chest, a crimson heart flanked by batwings. Veronica knew there were tattoos underneath the vest and ripped jeans, on her stomach, back and legs; Maisy had been a one-to-one client in the past and no doubt would be again. Veronica enjoyed the time shared with Maisy in submissive mode, and though they would never discuss it in public, Maisy's attitude to Veronica, ever since their first session, was one of friendly deference.

Maisy rushed to aid her.

"What can we do for you today, Madame?" She *always* called her Madame, in public or behind closed doors. She followed Veronica's gaze to the knee-high vinyl boots she had her eyes on. They were platformed and had six inches of heel beneath the creaking material and wide brims that would flare over her knees. "Oh, very nice choice, they'd look great on you. Try them on?"

"Soon," Veronica smiled. "Along with the rest of it."

Maisy followed her dutifully, picking up items as Veronica endorsed them, dropping them into a basket: a pair of fishnet holdups that would complement the footwear; a pair of fingerless latex gloves that would seal her arms all the way to the elbow, black to match the boots; and a black leather collar studded with steel points, fitted with a small metal hoop to which was joined a five-foot chain. Maisy's mind clearly wandered with each new item, dressing her Madame in her imagination and picturing the resulting goddess enslaving her as during their sessions.

"I need a corset. Any ideas?"

Maisy's eyes lit up to be asked her opinion. "We just got a new delivery this morning; we have something that would go with this perfectly. I'll be right back." She handed Veronica her basket and scurried away into the stockroom, allowing her Madame to drift through the store.

Veronica plucked a pair of handcuffs from the shelves. She had no concrete plan for tonight; this was not something a customer had asked for, so there was no stringent schedule to which she would have to adhere. Tonight would be organic, almost improvisational, so the canvas was blank and ripe with potential. A vibrating butt plug found its way into her basket alongside bottles of lubricant. A pair of steel handcuffs and fluffy counterparts joined them.

Then she came to a rack loaded with female-oriented toys, vibrators and dildos in all shapes, colours and sizes, knowing what she was looking for and certain of the final purchase the moment her eyes fell upon it.

She was snapped from her reverie by Maisy's excited return. "What do you think?"

The girl was holding a corset up to her own body, and she had been right: it was perfect. It was leather rather than latex, a duller sheen than the boots but one that spoke of craftsman ship and class. Suspender clips hung from its waist-cinching bottom, it had eyelets down the spine for tight lacing, and a zip running from between the bustier-shaped breast plates all the way to the navel, meaning it could be put on and taken off from front or back.

"I love it."

Maisy looked delighted with herself. "Anything else I can get you, Madame?"

"Yes," Veronica said, and her attention returned to the box emblazoned with the image of the figure hugging leather harness, threaded through with a seven inch rubber appendage that she pictured burrowing into Mark with every capable thrust of her hips. "I'll take that too."

*

Pulse's changing rooms were incredible, each one lined on two sides with red velvet curtains, fitted with a leather-padded bench for sitting, and two full length mirrors on opposite sides for optimum admiration of one's new sensual self, cascading away to infinity. It was like being in a never-ending tunnel of one's own vivacious sexuality.

Veronica dressed to ensure everything fit. She could hear Maisy on the other side of the entry veil, loitering, shuffling from foot to foot, keeping one eye on the shop but ever present in case her Madame required her. She was bold enough to ask.

"Do you need any help?"

Veronica smiled. Should she treat herself to a little promotional work? Looking at her reflection, clad in her new outfit, she felt wicked and indulgent.

"Why not?"

The curtain went back and Maisy made a move to enter, but was stopped in her tracks by the stunning sight. The boots, the latex gloves and the leather corset which did indeed suit her so wonderfully well, looked so *right* upon Veronica. Her reddish hair hung in a free cascade over her shoulders, leading the eye down to the cups of the corset, the zip, all the way down to dark panties.

"You look incredible, Madame," Maisy said huskily, her mind clearly on other things.

"I think the corset could be tighter, don't you?" Veronica said, and turned her back to allow Maisy to adjust it. The shorter girl gently swept Veronica's hair over her shoulder, and Veronica could feel her breath on the exposed skin of her back. She felt goose pimples rise across her upper arms, her forearms unable to bristle against the tight latex that sealed them. In the infinite reflection she watched Maisy bite her lower lip, half in concentration and half in lust, as she tugged at the cords across Veronica's spine. She inhaled languidly as the bodice squeezed tighter, and with nimble fingers Maisy tied off the strings to hold the cinched garment in place.

Veronica spun quickly and raised a boot, placing it against the padded seat between Maisy and the exit, ostensibly trapping the shop girl, though Veronica knew she would have no real desire to escape, regardless of her protestations.

"I think I have a customer," the girl murmured, pretending not to be startled and delighted by the sudden movement.

"They'll wait," Miss Veronica said coolly, looking down from the extra height provided by her new boots. Maisy's piercing green eyes looked away, as if to hold her Madame's gaze was heresy. "I want to see you again soon, Maisy. There's so much fun we've yet to have."

With a slow but decisive motion Veronica slipped a hand into Maisy's hair and drew her head back like a vampire exposing a succulent treat. She leaned in closer so Maisy could feel her hot breath on the naked flesh of her tattooed chest and pristine throat. Exposed fingers trailed down across her stomach, circling the navel piercing beneath her vest then down to the warm dale of her denim-clad quim. Veronica cupped her hand there and Maisy backed against the mirror, pinned in the corner, unable and unwilling to flee.

Veronica planted a delicate kiss against Maisy's throat and another on her jaw line. "Can I trust we'll see each other again soon, Maisy, my dear?"

Maisy whimpered with titillation and squirmed as Miss Veronica flexed her fingers against her sheathed box. "Yes, Madame. I want to be yours again."

Veronica pushed her body against her prey, feeling the heat radiating from her. She placed the briefest of kisses on her crimson lips, so gentle that Maisy could never be sure it had actually happened.

"I look forward to it."

Then she dropped her leg, freeing Maisy from capture and ushered her swiftly out of the booth before Maisy could be entirely sure what had occurred. Veronica tugged the curtain closed, alone in the room once more, unable to quell a broad smile.

It was a marketing tactic; always leave them wanting more, and now she knew for sure that an existing and repeat customer would be making another booking.

*

Veronica was quickly back in her everyday garb and the purchases were processed and paid for. "Somebody's going to be very lucky," Maisy said, and seemed incapable of meeting her Madame's eye.

"They certainly are," Veronica said with an aloof quality that she knew would drive the punk-pixie quietly wild. "Thank you for your help today."

She gave Maisy the faintest suggestion of a smile, thanked her and bade farewell, leaving the younger girl to watch her go in awe, and with a certainty of again seeking out the carnal pleasures only Miss Veronica could provide.

4

Steam roiled into the bedroom as Veronica opened the bathroom door and emerged wrapped in a towel. She padded across to her vanity table and poured herself a glass of the zinfandel she had set out to breathe before bathing. The rich burgundy liquid warmed her as it vanished from the glass. She threw on a playlist of relaxed chill out music. This was always how she began preparations for meeting a client: with calm. No matter how rowdy an evening would get, it started with gradual and unhurried prep.

Her routine getting ready for a one-to-one session rarely varied, regardless of the service she offered. First was a bath to shave her legs and her nethers, followed by a swift hot shower, rinsing away any soapy water. Then was her glass of wine; she never overdid it, because it was imperative to keep her wits sharp, but it helped the process, the assuming of the role of Miss Veronica. While very much a part of her, it still felt like slipping on a costume, of allowing her darkest passions free reign. What came next often felt like Miss Veronica taking over, gradually assuming control as each part of her appearance was constructed.

She shrugged the towel off completely, admiring herself in the mirror. She was pale skinned, reedy and slender. She liked her small breasts and their perky nipples, and though she would often wish they were bigger, she soon forgot her desires when she laid eyes on the bubble-like perfection of her ass. It was her best and favourite asset, and she would jokingly brag about it in conversation, but her love for her posterior was genuine, as was that of all the men who lavished and worshipped it on demand.

She began.

Veronica had a number of hairstyles she adopted when not specified by clients, and her favourite was the braid held in place by a black and silver clip, something which would complement her chosen outfit perfectly. She coiled strands of her hair around one another in an elaborate plat, hanging it over her shoulder and examining every fold, every curl, until it was secured into place with the clip. It traced a perfect line down her naked spine.

Then came her makeup; she very rarely wore a lot in her more mundane day to day, but Miss Veronica liked dark, smoky eyes and a darker shade of lipstick. Veronica applied everything with a cool method, until she stared at a reflection whose eyes were now alive with promise and danger, lips a subtler shade of the wine she sipped.

Now came her outfit, and she savoured every action of dressing. She rolled on the fishnet stockings, relishing the feel of the woven threads against her flesh and the band clinging at her thigh. Next she pulled on the gloves, and it felt like dipping her arms into cool tar as they bonded to her; she flexed her fingers, knitting them together until they were on tightly, and she was amazed at how instantly they felt a part of her. Her white digits stood out in contrast against ebony palms.

She laced the back of the corset as tightly as it would go, slipping into it like armour, a leather carapace which hugged her form. It had been fun to have Maisy to help earlier, but she was more than capable of it herself. She inhaled deeply and tugged it tight across her stomach and chest and zipped it up, sealing herself within.

The boots went on with a measured effort, and she mastered the necessary new gait within moments. She found it altered the way she moved, the way she felt; the new roll to her hips made her feel like she was stalking down prey, and it gave her a new air of power and control.

Veronica looked at herself in the mirror once more, and Miss Veronica stared back. Behind those eyes she was hungry for what lay ahead, plotting the sexual ruination of the man who would enter her chambers within the next half hour. She ran her hands across her latex-wrapped forearms, the faultless corset, and into the basin of her shaven sex, still unclothed, the way it would remain. Her pussy would be exposed, a constant tease, begging for his touch, but he would be forbidden from laying even a fingertip against it.

With the clock ticking until his arrival she sent a message to Phoebe, turned on her computer, and within a few minutes her friend's face appeared in her webcam chat program; Phoebe was ready for the evening, sprawled on her bed, clad in a silk gown, her own wine in hand. Her mouth fell open when she saw what Veronica was wearing.

"Oh my heavens, you look incredible," she gasped.

"You approve?"

"Girl, I'm imagining being your toy for tonight instead of him! Mark will love it."

"I don't care if he loves it or not, he has no say in the matter," she said with a grin. "I'll be turning off the monitor and muting the sound so we won't be able to see or hear you, but you'll be able to hear every word we say."

There was a knock at the door. Veronica glanced at the clock to see it was precisely seven o'clock. At least he had listened.

"Give him hell, tigress."

She shut down vision and volume, and took the final breath, giving Miss Veronica control. She strode to the front door of the flat and opened it, revealing Mark standing in smart trousers and a shirt. He was maintaining composure, but his whole demeanour altered when he laid eyes on her. He attempted to speak but no words came.

She spoke for him.

"In. Now."

*

Mark looked as if he didn't know what to do, moving quietly into the bedroom, unsure of what to say, how to stand. Veronica strode in behind him, hands on hips. The distant thoughts of her nerves were thrust away and she looked him up and down, projecting aloof disdain with practiced skill.

"So, you came. I must admit I thought you'd chicken out at the last minute and spend the night on your own, wallowing in your misery and interfering with yourself."

A smart comment threatened to appear but he swallowed it. "No."

"No?" she repeated sharply.

"No, Miss Veronica."

"Better," she said, and circled him like a vulture around helpless carrion, tracking a finger across his chest, shoulders and back. It thrilled her to be touching him like this when she knew Phoebe could see everything. The thought of it made every fibre inside her tingle, her best friend getting off on seeing the man whom had never lit a spark within her reduced to a plaything. She had not even begun and she knew it was a feeling she would chase again, perhaps as a new service, now that she knew there was a willing market for it. She looked him square in the eyes. "Do you like my outfit?"

"It's lovely," he said, looking her up and down, a lascivious smirk growing on his face. She slapped it away; not hard enough to truly hurt, but stinging enough to shock. She wouldn't let him argue, and clutched his jaw and cheeks with one hand.

"What do you think you're doing? How dare you look at me like I'm a piece of meat, here for your pleasure? You're here to entertain me, not the other way around, is that clear?"

There wasn't fear in his eyes; it was alarm and subdued, emasculated anger. She had struck a chord. It took him a few seconds, but he nodded.

"Is that clear?" she persisted.

"Yes, Miss Veronica," he said through squeezed lips, and she slapped him gently upon release.

"Good, boy. Good."

Gloved hands went to his chest, feeling the musculature beneath his shirt, or lack thereof; he was toned, but far from the pinnacle of perfection. "Hmm, you don't spend a lot of time in the gym, do you?" She circled him again, and her hands went to the meat of his buttocks, feeling the lack of definition. "And you spend more time sitting on this arse playing your little games and touching yourself, don't you? How does it feel knowing you were never man enough for your girl? No wonder she got rid of you."

"Well, she —"

Another moderate slap, with a flick of fingers rather than a palm. It hushed him.

She pouted theatrically and affected a mocking voice. "Oh, touched a nerve, have I?" She lifted his arms, noted the small moist stains at his armpits. "You're nervous, are you? Another sign of weakness. Take that shirt off boy; you should be ashamed of yourself."

He unbuttoned and dropped it to the floor. She kicked it aside with a boot and appraised his naked torso. There was little extra fat there; it was a body he kept thin, but did very little extra to maintain. She tweaked his right nipple, causing a sharp, hissing intake of breath.

"You're just a sack of undefined flesh. You have no idea what appeals to women, do you? No idea how to satisfy one? And don't say 'I've had no complaints before' because we all know how much of a lie that is. If you knew what you were doing you wouldn't be here. Now take off your shoes, socks and trousers, in that order."

"Yes, Miss Veronica."

He obeyed in silence, slipping off shoes and stuffing them with socks. As he did so Veronica retreated a few steps with the pretence of watching, but her hand went behind her and opened the top drawer of the chest, delving into her box of tricks, feeling for the tool she knew was there, latex-clad hand closing around the sturdy handle.

Mark unbuckled his trousers and slid them down, baring himself completely to her; he was already beginning to stiffen, seven inches of thick meat bobbing before him as it made the journey to full erectness. He let out a startled gasp when the tip of a riding crop swept between his legs and traced across his scrotum and along the underside of his cock, coaxing it harder. He followed the length of the crop up across the latex of her gloves, across her pale shoulder to her eyes.

"I've seen far bigger boy, no wonder you haven't a clue how to satisfy a woman."

She flicked the stiff whip against his thighs, watching his jaw set with tension. As she increased the strength of her strokes she watched his hands move to stop her. He knew the safeword, and if he wasn't prepared to use it then she would tolerate no rebellion. "Hands off, you don't stop me from doing a thing. Understand?"

"Yes, Miss Veronica," he said through gritted teeth.

"Now turn around." He did so gingerly, looking back over his shoulder to see what she had planned. "Eyes forward, boy!" His head snapped back into position. "Good. Now bend over. Those who disobey get punished."

She whipped the inside of his thighs until he spread his feet apart, then he pivoted at the waist, hands pressed flat against the bed, backside thrust up and out for her. She laughed at him, ensuring a cruel undertone. "Oh, don't you look a treat, all pale and exposed. You need a good whipping, don't you boy?"

"Yes, Miss Veronica," he said.

"Then let's begin."

*

Phoebe lay on the bed with her laptop beside her, the screen displaying the real-time happenings within Miss Veronica's chamber. She watched Mark enter, still not entirely certain of the manner he should adopt and soon educated to be subservient. She giggled as Veronica berated him, winced as she slapped him, and felt a pang of righteous fulfillment when he was forced to strip down to his skin.

She was rubbing her breasts through the silken material of her gown, and pulled it open to allow easier access to the naked flesh beneath. She tweaked her nipples as she watched Mark get into position, and her best friend take up a spot behind him, flexing the riding crop in preparation for its next job.

Even across the data connection, she heard the *whoosh* it made as it sliced the air.

*

Miss Veronica brought the crop down harder than she had intended, and it made a satisfying slap as it rippled the flesh of Mark's right buttock. He let out a hiss of air through clenched teeth.

"Oh, sorry my little darling, was that too hard?"

His response surprised her: "No, Miss Veronica. Not too hard at all."

Perhaps he was being tough, showing off; she brought a stroke down with equal force across his left cheek and got the same response, but the third strike, back across the exact spot she had laid the first, brought an audible and deep cry of pain. The area had already reddened, a delicate welt rising.

"That one surprised you, didn't it?"

"Yes, Miss Veronica," he managed with a shortness of breath, steeling himself against her next onslaught. She eased her strokes somewhat, knowing that each subsequent one would hurt more than the last now they were lashing tender flesh. As her elbow repeated its motions she looked towards the blank monitor, directly at the webcam and gave a sultry smile, imagining the look of delight on Phoebe's face as she watched this.

"Oh, poor little baby, no clue what to do to please a lady, isn't that right? Eleven stone of wasted meat with a feeble cock attached."

She laid the crop to rest across his back and kicked his legs further apart to off-balance him and force his face into the soft mattress. A hand reached over and under until it found his penis, still somewhere between full arousal and rest. She stroked it gently, never gripping, but coaxing it slowly to its full potential. With her other hand she trailed a fingertip down the dell of his buttocks, prying them open to find his naked and intimate entrance, cleaned and prepared for her. His cock bucked against her latex palm and she allowed him a brief moment of pleasure, closing her fist around it.

"Oh, does that feel good?" she said, and he moaned his approval.

"It feels fucking great," he began, and with a flash she broke contact with his dick and snatched up the crop, bringing it across the outside of his thighs and the back of his knees. They almost buckled.

"Watch that foul language with me boy, do you hear me?" she barked venomously. "I reserve the right to speak like that but I won't be spoken to in that manner, least of all in my own home, do you understand?"

"Yes, Miss," he mewled. "I'm sorry, I'm so sorry."

"On your knees, right now."

She administered an additional lash to each leg to speed up his descent. With a thud and a cry he hit the deck and she grabbed a handful of his hair, jerking his head back and ensuring he looked directly into her eyes. "If you behave like an animal we'll treat you like one."

Veronica went back to her drawer and she pulled out the collar and chain she had bought at *Pulse*, running the silver links between her fingers. Mark offered his throat and she threaded the collar around and fastened it below his Adam's apple. He was fully able to breathe, but a tug of the chain brought a roughhoused gasp.

"You see what happens boy? Now beg for me to continue like a good little doggy."

This almost looked like it would be too much for him, but his arms rose before him, mimicking a canine seeking affection, and he said: "Please, Miss Veronica. Please continue." There was an earnest look in his eyes and she couldn't help but laugh.

"Come on, pet, let's go for a walk."

He obeyed, crawling behind as she led him around the room, skirting the edge of the bed before sprawling herself on the silk sheets and opening her legs to present him for the first time with her cloven treat, bare and glistening with her own excitement. His eyes went to it momentarily, then quickly returned to meet her gaze.

"Looks delicious, doesn't it?" she said, and reeled in the chain, hand over hand, drawing his face closer to her snatch. He looked pleased, ready to indulge in something a little more vanilla, something he fully understood. Or indeed, not *fully*, for otherwise he would not be here.

Mark was inches away when she put a boot against his shoulder, digging the point of her heel against his pectoral muscle and pushing him back, denying him the taste of her. She nodded her head towards her footwear.

"Boots. Clean them, doggy."

Mark deflated but did as instructed, tongue emerging and trailing in awkward lines across the latex, expression souring as he tasted the tartness of brand new PVC, undoubtedly for the first time. Miss

Veronica smiled with gratitude, coiling the chain around her forearm to ensure he could not pull too far away.

It felt incredible. Not the sensation of his tongue, because that was impossible to sense through her boots, but the feeling of control and power over him. It was so potently different to her usual one-to-one sessions, where the client paid for their submissive fantasies to be conjured into reality; no matter how subservient they became they still had the ultimate control, because they were procuring a service. Here, now, this was all her, a side of herself she had rarely, if indeed ever, tapped before. It was revelatory, and she realised it was not entirely Miss Veronica running the show but her true self; the girl who had grown up unassuming, even shy, who had channeled an exaggerated version of herself to indulge her darker desires and found it made her a good living. She was not Miss Veronica, a role, but merely Veronica unleashed, and it sent her heart thundering, mind swimming with possibilities.

She adored this power but would relish a reversal, to allow herself to be controlled. In her darker dreams she often imagined throwing herself at the mercy of another, to be used as they saw fit. More snippets of last night's drunken conversations came back to her; the things she told her friend she would love to try, fantasies she had yet to achieve.

She would seek that unbridled feeling of total surrender, but not tonight. Tonight was for Phoebe, and she shot another look towards the webcam, a look that spoke of hunger and joy.

*

Phoebe's laptop was sat evenly between her knees. Her robe was shed now, bundled beneath her bare flesh, pert nipples casting long shadows across her breasts in the luminous glow from the computer screen. She fondled her tits with one hand, tweaking the dark buds, while her other hand pleasured the folds of flesh between her thighs. She was so aroused and open down below, pink and glistening with dew.

Mark cleaned Veronica's incredible boots with his tongue and her best friend gazed down the lens directly at her. It was like they were in the room, and Veronica's voice was crystal clear.

"What a waste of a good tongue," she told Mark. "Poor Phoebe wanted it to give the same care and attention to her pussy, you know. Every waking hour. What kind of man refuses to devote himself entirely to the pleasure of his lady? A pathetic specimen, indeed."

Phoebe felt a climax approaching with nerve-shaking alacrity. She sank two fingers into herself, tending to her clit with the heel of her hand, relishing the moist sounds that accompanied Veronica's voice.

"You do a reasonable job. Let's see how you handle my puckered little hole..."

Veronica added some slack to the chain for as long as it took her to roll onto all fours, parallel to the camera so Phoebe could marvel at her posture. Then, with the chain over her shoulder like a worker hauling in cargo, she pulled Mark's face into the cleft of her ass. Mark made a muffled grunt as his head moved between Veronica's cheeks; she reached back and pried them wider to allow him to breathe, and with perfect clarity Phoebe watched Mark's tongue tend to the perfect round button of Veronica's asshole.

*

Veronica couldn't control the noise that burst from her, wholly satisfied moan. She pulled the leash tighter and forced herself back against him, allowing his tongue to worm its way a few centimetres past the threshold of her most sacred orifice. Whenever he tried to sink lower to lick her second hole she angled herself to keep him at bay and pulled his chain tighter.

This was as far as she'd ever gone with anal pleasure, and this the first time in years; the first time was an accident, when her partner had been so drunk he hadn't realised what he was doing, instantly recoiling upon discovering just where his tongue had been. She was ever reluctant to break the seal of that final sanctuary with anything larger or firmer than the probing wet muscle now seeking entry, but the thought of breaking that taboo was ever present. It was ironic, the things she did, and her willingness to do it to men and women if they asked, but she had never made that final leap to try it for herself.

She unleashed him and slid like mercury across the bed and back to the drawer, slipping out a pair of steel handcuffs, ignoring the fluffy ones completely; tonight was not a night for comfort.

"On the bed on all fours," she demanded, positioning him to be sideways-on for their distant audience. She pulled his hands behind his back and slapped the cuffs around his wrists, the collar-chain allowing her to keep his face lifted from the sheets, ever tensed and controlling. Still at the drawer she removed the black torpedo of the vibrating butt plug and a bottle of lubricant.

"Phoebe tells me you seem interested the thought of having your ass toyed... pegged... fucked senseless."

He surrendered to the admission. "Yes, Miss. I do."

"Why?" she asked, popping the cap from the lube and dribbling some of the silken liquid across the black jelly rubber surface, smearing it with her fingers.

"I don't know Miss. I just...thought it would be fun. A little different and a little naughty."

"You sad fool," Veronica said. "That girl would have *thrived* on different and naughty. You never even considered asking her?"

Veronica pressed the narrow cone of the plug against Mark's anus and twisted the small dial at the base, activating the vibrating mechanism. Mark instantly bristled and let out a nervous laugh.

"I suppose I didn't want to freak her out. I've never wanted to freak her out."

It was a surprisingly sweet sentiment; a man afraid that revealing his desires would alarm or offend, so he kept them inside. If Phoebe was in search of an explanation, it was the closest she would get. Veronica looked at the camera, wondering how Phoebe took that news, if indeed it was news to her.

*

Phoebe's second orgasm built more gradually this time, and hearing Mark's words changed nothing. She was desperate to see him with that butt plug inside him, desperate to see what would come next. The fingers of one hand stretched her pliant labia while the slick digits of the other thrummed against her clit. She couldn't resist lapping her nectar from her fingers before plunging them back into herself. Her body glimmered with a sheen of sweat in the light of the laptop.

Veronica returned to the task at hand, twisting the plug and allowing it to burrow into the slave boy's hole. His body stiffened against the foreign object but Phoebe could see the pleasure on his face. With a slow moan he took it all, the cone widening towards the base before narrowing sharply again; Phoebe saw the plug snatched from Veronica's hand as Mark's ass took it past its widest point and brought it within him.

"Good boy!" Veronica said with genuine approval and Phoebe felt waves of pleasure intensify, burst and dissipate throughout her, far gentler but no less wonderful than her first climax. There would be more to come, and she wanted each one to be different.

Veronica left the butt plug to do its joy-spreading work and returned to her drawer for the final item. She stepped gracefully into the harness and drew it up across her thighs; it was a simple but sturdy construct of leather that looped across her buttocks and hips, with a triangular segment with a circular hole that rested against her pussy. Before she pulled it tight she fitted the *piece de resistance*; a six inch black jelly rubber dong, realistically moulded to resemble an actual dick. It slid through the o-ring and was tugged flush against the shaven flesh just above her kitty, leaving that haven exposed. Veronica tightened the straps and strutted around to the other side of the bed so Mark could get a good look.

"Fuck me..." he gasped in surprise, body clearly alive with the sensation of the buzzing toy inside him.

Veronica smiled. "Oh, I intend to boy."

5

Veronica took the chain into her hand again and sauntered back to Mark's posterior. She took hold of the butt plug and withdrew it slowly, watching the muscle of his ass distend but remain flush with the contours of the retreating toy. He made a satisfied groan as the device unsheathed inch-by-inch until his tight asshole was free again, quivering, waiting for something bigger.

"You're going to enjoy this, aren't you?" Veronica asked.

"Yes, Miss Veronica, I'm going to love it." Any modicum of hesitation was gone from his tone completely; he was here in the moment and desperate to be owned. "Fuck me, please, I beg you."

"You beg me? I like that."

She uncapped the lubricant and dribbled a sizeable trickle across Mark's butt cheeks and into the vale between, smearing it around his eager hole and slipping in a finger without resistance. More lube coated the dong bobbing between them until it was slick and ready.

Veronica was alive with the wonder of it, free and unleashed and able to be herself. She remembered why she had ventured into this world in the first place. The money was not reason enough; she loved this, loved the feeling of sexual energy, of controlling and being in charge and being worshipped by people. Men, women, it didn't matter.

"Fuck me, *please*," Mark insisted, and she would deny him no longer.

With the chain around her wrist she clutched his hip for extra leverage and pushed the bulbous tip of the dong against his ass. It opened without hesitation and she sank slowly into him, expecting resistance and receiving none. He cried out with a mix of ecstasy and pain but the line between them was nonexistent. Within seconds the rubber cock was in him up to the root and she clutched his other hip, marveling at the force with which he bucked back to meet her.

"Oh, all the way in on the first try! Something tells me you're not a stranger to this..."

"Oh fuck me, please, take me hard," Mark panted.

Veronica slid the strap-on from him and back in, reaming his hole with each gliding thrust. She started slowly at first but soon built to a quick rhythm; the sound of her thighs slapping against him filled the room along with his pleasured grunting.

"You're a sissy little fucktoy, aren't you? This is why you couldn't satisfy Phoebe, you'd much rather be on the receiving end of a dick."

Veronica spat into his ass to add to the cocktail of lubricating fluid. She released his hips and now clutched both the collar chain and the links of the handcuffs across his back and tugged on them, arching his back further until only his knees remained on the bed. He was hers now, her property, and she bucked into him with all the might she had. She had done this before to paying clients, including to Maisy the shop girl, but never with such freeing fervour.

She wanted to see his face, see the fruits of her labours etched onto that sweating visage. "On your back, boy."

She withdrew and he collapsed, rolling over clumsily with his arms trapped underneath him. His cock was swollen to a staggering degree, veins bulging, head purple and raw, balls tight.

"Oh, you *are* enjoying it."

She forced down on his thighs, splaying them, holding them flat and uncomfortably wide as she navigated the dong into him again, surveying his expression as it changed from anticipation to pain to pleasure with every new millimetre of rubber mass that delved within. Veronica used his cock almost as a levering post, clutching it with no intention of letting go and pushing into him.

"Oh, that's good boy, take it all. Good little slave."

With some pressure the chain levered him off the bed again, arms useless beneath him, and his face flushed red with exertion. Her own chest had reddened, nipples scraping against the inside of the corset cups. The warmth in her pussy radiated out through her body, tingling with delight despite remaining untouched.

His cock looked primed to come but he had a surprising amount of stamina. It was criminal that he wasn't a better lover, and that he had wasted so much of Phoebe's time, because it was the kind of cock that could bring endless pleasure if wielded by someone with a sliver of skill or a fraction of interest. Her gaze bored into his, their faces inches away. He allowed himself a smile.

She wanted to see him come, see the fruits of her labours manifest in a squirting geyser of seed. "Let's let your hands loose from behind your back, shall we? Perhaps chain you to the headboard and finish you off."

"Yes Miss Veronica, anything you say," he said, with a gleam of mischief in his eyes. She paid it no mind and withdrew the dong from him. He panted breathlessly as she retrieved the key from the drawer and rolled him over, unlocking the steel cuffs and allowing him to massage his wrists and flex his elbows and shoulders. It was likely to be the tension, but perhaps her imagination, that brought out every muscle beneath his skin, and for the first time he looked surprisingly powerful.

One of those arms shot out and clutched her by the back of the neck, strong enough that it made her yelp.

Her first instinct was to lash out and punch him but she quelled it, mind racing with the possibilities of what was occurring, voice silenced by the hungry look in his eyes. He twisted her 180 degrees and brought her arms together, snatching the handcuffs from her grip and securing them onto her wrists with unbeatable speed. He tugged her close to him and she felt the engorged length of his cock against her bare ass cheeks.

His whispering voice was husky in her ear and sent a shiver through her.

"My turn."

*

Phoebe had reached another level of orgasmic bliss as she watched Mark being fucked with such passion, every expression on his face a blend of discomfort and delight. The sheets beneath her were soaked with sweat, and a dark stain between her thighs was a musky reminder of her thrill. But the best was yet to come.

Her pulse quickened further when Veronica unbound Mark, and after stretching out he took her in hand and restrained her. She could have screamed, lashed out, but she held firm, just as Phoebe knew she would. The split second Veronica reacted negatively Mark would stop, just as planned, but Veronica appeared more than willing to explore what was happening.

With the cuffs in place, Mark marched her to the desk on which her computer stood and angled her body so her face filled Phoebe's screen. He turned on the monitor and sound, and Veronica's expression changed to indicate that she could see Phoebe once more.

"Hi there gorgeous," she purred. "The fact you haven't screamed blue murder confirms what I thought. You play the role of mistress and you're always worried to be submissive, but you want it more than anything. Every time we get drunk and talk dirty you mention it, and I was a little tired of seeing that fine little body of yours go to waste. It deserves to be used and mistreated. You deserve to get what you want. So I told Mark and we decided to give you a gift."

Veronica processed this. "So you're not broken up?"

"Alas, my lady, that part's not a lie, but it's totally mutual. Sometimes it just doesn't work out. No regrets. But lucky for you,

Mark's not the hopeless fuck I might have led you to believe, and I don't want to destroy your confidence but that isn't the first time he's had someone go to town on him with a strap-on."

Phoebe reached off the edge of the bed and retrieved the toy she had positioned there earlier for its eventual reveal. It was a six inch purple penis, quivering in her hand, attached to a similarly coloured harness. She slid the dong free from the o-ring.

"Naughty boy," Veronica said, and Mark's hand came around her mouth to silence her.

"The rules have changed, remember? We thought about just approaching you outright and suggesting this, but this way was far more fun. I'm really rather proud of myself. This one's from me, gorgeous. And, I suppose, *for* me too. I wanted to see you in action, and now I want to see you get ruined. We really need to be more adventurous."

She blew a kiss, and Veronica was pulled away from the screen and forced to bend over the bed while Mark took up a position behind her, the blade of his hand raised. He brought it down hard with a strident slap.

Veronica yelped, and Phoebe nestled the purple dildo into her quim to fully enjoy the show.

*

Veronica savoured the feeling of a hand raining open-palmed blows onto her ass, every one bringing a heavy dose of pain and a rush of exquisite gratification. She had so rarely been spanked before; she was always the one dishing out the domination. It was with such regularity that her own desires had been buried beneath the mask of Miss Veronica, allowed to blossom in the dark part of her mind, fed by the luminous light of experience and lust. Mark knew what he was doing too, and she no longer looked at him as a sexual failure, or even a deviant; he was merely comfortable and adventurous, and it made her lust for him, and want to further submit to him.

"How do you like it, slut?" she heard Phoebe's giggling voice say from the computer.

"It's – ah! – wonderful!"

She looked to see Phoebe on her screen, legs spread, plunging her toy into her sodden cunt, watching the goings-on within the bedroom with unbroken interest.

"Put the collar on her," Phoebe ordered. Mark unfastened it from his throat.

Veronica allowed him to fit her with the collar; it was tight against her throat, and it felt so good to be the one in thrall for a change. Finance and necessity had made her deny herself these pleasures; without intention, sex had become something she gave to other people, not embraced. No more. Her best friend indicated her approval in her typically garrulous fashion.

"Every time she gets a few drinks in her she talks about how much she wants to be the slave, to be whipped and nipped and owned. You'll barely remember anything you said on Friday, I bet, but this is it made real."

Mark walked the edge of the bed with leash in hand, leading her across the covers to the place she had discarded the riding crop. Her artificial member bobbed against her thighs.

He closed a fist around the handle and brandished it slowly, tracing the flog against her throat.

"Get her out of that corset," Phoebe demanded, and her now-silent enforcer obeyed, zipping the shell open. It was like a chrysalis falling away, Veronica a butterfly spreading her wings at last, pale skinned yet blindingly vibrant.

Mark grinned, and played the flog across her flat stomach and between her petite breasts. She released a nervous breath.

He flicked the crop against her torso and tummy, light enough for it to sting but not really hurt. All the while he looked at her, through her, with affection, lust and commanding control in those eyes, which she noticed for the first time were a rich chocolate brown. What he lacked in muscle mass was more than made up for in attitude.

Mark reached out and rolled her nipples between fingertips, and the instant her eyes closed to appreciate the feeling he pinched them, tweaked them, pulling pained yelps from her. It was wonderful.

"Bend her over, whip that perfect peachy ass," Phoebe ordered, a sex-crazed Big Brother watching from her control room, seeing the results of her backstage machinations. Veronica obliged and took a face-first plunge into the duvet as Mark pitched her forward. With her hands cuffed behind her back she couldn't support herself, and angled her head to be able to breathe. Mark hefted her hips upward, presenting the divine curve of her buttocks as a target to be struck.

"Brace yourself, doll," Phoebe said, and Veronica heard the slicing of the air from a position she had never heard it from before: the receiving end. It sounded *sharp*, and when the crop hit her cheeks she cried out.

"Fuck!" she howled, and started to laugh nervously in anticipation of the next strike. They came with an irregular rhythm so she could never fully prepare for them, and each one brought a slash of pain and heart-quickening pleasure.

And then with zero tenderness she felt Mark's free hand between her thighs, the edge of his hand trailing through the open furrow of her pussy, still slick with delight. A knuckle brushed her clit and her knees buckled, and then a finger slid within her tight walls, a thumb pushing against her ass.

The flogging stopped and she heard the pop of the lubricant bottle's cap, then shivered at the feeling of the cool liquid poured between her cheeks. Again with no prelude she felt the pad of his thumb press against her sacred hole and she involuntarily bucked forward, away from him, a look of nervous fear on her face. Phoebe saw it instantly and halted her own play, speaking soothingly.

"You talk about this all the time," Phoebe explained, and Veronica knew that was true. Doing it to others had planted the seed, growing with the rest of her submissive needs, spoken of when encouraged by alcohol and friendship. "Trust me, it's fun if you do it right. *Very* fun."

She eased herself back, reluctance still strong but tempered with curiosity. Mark knew to be more compassionate now and took care of her. The pad of his thumb returned to the forbidden pit and sought a more relaxed entrance, and with delicate pressure it started to slip within her.

Veronica gritted her teeth against the new visitor but it wasn't necessary. She felt more at ease and her hole welcomed the exploring digit. His deft fingers continued to massage her snatch as he guided his thumb deeper, and with a few seconds and the application of more oily fluid it was in as far as it could go.

It felt incredible. Her tight muscles clamped against him. The fire down below intensified, radiating out from her expertly-tended pussy;

he brought the digits together, and though separated by her inner walls he made a motion of rubbing thumb and forefinger together which triggered a sudden and unanticipated orgasm, shaking her whole body and momentarily blinding her to senses and logic. Her knees slipped off the bed and his fingers slipped out of her; she landed on the meat of her bottom, unable to stop herself, gasping, flushed red and sweating.

Phoebe called out with appreciation. "Good girl!" she said. "I told you."

Mark reached down to help her up, gripping the latex at her elbow. As sense returned, she realised she didn't want to be helped up. She wanted to be led.

She angled her head and thrust her neck towards him, eyes wide and willing. He took the hint immediately and closed his fist around the chain, tugging her back into position on the bed. She lowered her face again and threw a wink at Phoebe, who had resumed her play, quietly thrusting the toy within her.

A glance over her shoulder showed Mark pouring lube directly across his dick, stroking and smearing it to ensure a full coating. The head soon pushed against her defences and she eased back; it was harder this time, and did come with a modicum of pain, but with careful movements she felt her asshole spread for him and allow him inside; it snapped closed as it passed the rim of his pole's crown, and they merged as one. It wasn't pain now, just mild discomfort, eased by a copious volume of lube, and soon it was pleasure entirely. She felt complete, as if this had been missing for such a long time; not just the tool foraging within, building to a relentless rhythm, but the feeling of throwing herself open to her sexual wishes and thoughts. She dished it out so readily, and had always required to take it equally. The balance was found. This is what she would be from now on.

"Arch her back," Phoebe demanded, and the chain went taut, lifting Veronica's head from the bed. As she had done to him, Mark held her in position with both the chain and cuffs across her lower back and levered himself deeper into her. He was virtually silent throughout, the occasional grunt escaping his lips as his naked cock fucked her ass, the tight canal accommodating with skill. It was Phoebe who provided the encouragement throughout.

"Good girl," she gasped. "Such a naughty girl. You love it, don't you?"

"I do," she breathed. "Please, sir, play with my pussy."

Phoebe laughed. "Don't deny her."

Mark let the chain go and reached around to tend to her dripping box, tickling her clit and pushing fingers into her, swiftly conducting her to crescendo. She felt briefly weightless, her head swimming, and a detonation occurred in her pussy that she had never felt the equal of. It was mix of two orgasms brought on by the new and old sensations, and it blindsided her. Tears prickled her eyes and she screamed loud enough to rouse the whole street, but she didn't care. She *couldn't* care. She could merely exist here, beyond the world, swaddled by and filled with burning passion and lust.

Distantly she heard Phoebe climax, howling her joy as she came in unison with her friend. Then Mark was out of her and the chain went slack, so that she fell back to the duvet, drawing in ragged breaths. Her master was not quite done and she felt his sturdy hand on her neck, holding her down despite the fact she couldn't muster resistance even if she had wanted to. Her final act of submission was to take his seed.

He came with a rasping grunt, arcs of glistening white nectar pumping across her cheeks and trickling down across her lips, anointed by his gift like a true submissive. She opened her mouth to allow in rivulets of cum, to baste her tongue with salt, and she licked at the pool that formed on her sheets. He caressed her hair as she lapped up his offering, savouring every drop as if it were a reward, and all the while she watched Phoebe on her monitor.

Her friend smiled warmly, clearly filled with the sensation of a job well done. She looked sated, content and proud.

*

Mark uncuffed her, dressed quickly and left without another word. She would realise later it was the last time she or Phoebe would ever see him; he remained local and they heard of him through mutual friends, but their paths never crossed again.

When she was able, Veronica drew herself up and stood, still clad in her mistress attire and adorned with the strap-on. She laughed, almost self-consciously, as Phoebe watched her while tugging on her robe. Veronica did the same, feeling the sweat on her body drying with a chill.

Veronica flopped into her chair and came face to face with her friend. She poured herself another glass of wine from the long-forgotten bottle and let the liquid fill her; its warmth was nothing compared to the sensations of satisfaction left by what she had just experienced.

"Look at you, the sexual mastermind," Veronica smiled. "That was a very risky gamble."

"I know you better than you know yourself. You've wanted this for so long and I saw a perfect opportunity to give it to you. Believe me, it was a hell of a show."

"So that's it, then," Veronica smiled. "You've finally seen me at work."

Phoebe laughed. "And you're so ridiculously good at your job. All that's left is to experience it firsthand."

There was a silence between them; not awkward, but a quiet agreement, that perhaps there was one part of their friendship left to explore and they may very well get to it now that the boundaries had been brought down.

That's precisely how Veronica felt. Boundless and free. She understood herself, understood what Miss Veronica had been; an exaggeration of herself, a costume, a mask.

She would not need to wear the mask anymore.

CLOSING TIME AT PULSE

It was the longest shift of Maisy Porter's life.

What had started as an uneventful day at *Pulse*, the region's classiest and most high-end sex shop, had become alive with sexual excitement, all due to an appearance by Madame Veronica, who had been shopping for toys and an outfit with which to pleasure a mystery client. Maisy was filled with jealousy at the thought of Veronica with someone else, a ludicrous notion since her Madame was a professional cam-queen, mistress, dominatrix, or whatever one paid her for, but it still riled her to think of the exquisite strawberry blonde goddess working her unmitigated magic and skills on another eager patron.

Maisy, five foot three of boundless energy, a punk-pixie with shoulder length hair vibrant with neon red dye, pale skin glowing with the colour of dozens of tattoos, could concentrate no longer, not since she had ventured into the changing room to assist her Madame in lacing up a leather corset, then to have the domineering princess pin her against the wall, cup Maisy's seeping wetness through her jeans and flex fingers that had given Maisy so many crippling orgasms before. Her knees had almost given out, heart racing, mind flooding with submissive thoughts and the need to be taken there in the cubicle, in the ever-dwindling spiral of the infinity mirror, but Veronica had denied her, planting kisses on her throat and lips and insisting Maisy come visit her soon.

She had served Madame Veronica her goods and watched her walk out with her usual confident stride, and Maisy knew she would see her this week. Her panties were moistened so that every step she took was a reminder of the power the lady had over her; her febrile labia brushed against the sodden gusset within tight denim, swollen clit rubbing against moist material. She needed release; it wouldn't be the first time she had done so at work, but the world conspired against her and was determined to keep her on the precipice of joy.

Customers kept appearing, emerging from the cold to tread the hardwood floors and peruse the racks for a new tool or garment that would fill their life with excitement. Maisy couldn't believe it. Didn't these people have jobs or homes to go to? How dare they come here, to a *shop*, with the intention of *buying things*? With her own needs to attend to, theirs were selfish. She caught the thought, giggling at her own fuzzy thinking, blurred by the desperate need to come, but it didn't change the fact. From the moment her Madame had strutted from the emporium there was never a period where she was alone; customers came and went, always overlapping. At three PM a large order arrived and Maisy spent the rest of her shift, between serving a diverse parade of men and women their lingerie and handcuffs and lubricants, processing, cataloguing and shelving the new stock. Every new toy she hung she pictured vanishing into her pussy; it now thrummed with a distant ache, desperation having gradually faded as the hours wore on, but it was ever-present, humid and deprived.

The shift ground endlessly on until the clock closed in on five o'clock. She had eaten a swift lunch at the counter and hadn't even had time for a coffee or cigarette break all day; it wasn't rare that she worked Saturdays alone, but her lack of a good orgasm when so desperately required had left her feeling hard-done to and likely to complain to Maxwell, *Pulse's* owner, when next she saw him.

Don't be silly, girl. You'll have bust your nut a dozen times before then and you'll be thinking straight.

She thought less of Veronica now and more of Reece, who would be coming to meet her as soon as her shift ended, and they'd head out for food, drinks and a night of abandon. Saturday night was always wild, just the way she liked it, filled with drinking, dancing, and throwing herself open to pleasure, vice and sin.

Reece arrived three minutes early. He had a tousled mop of jet black hair and piercing blue eyes, rimmed as usual with eyeliner to make them pop irresistibly. Ever the emo poster-boy, he wore a tight fitting band T-shirt that hugged his skinny, fatless frame, every muscle like a knot in wire. He had spiked leather straps around his wrists and black fishnet gauntlets up to his elbows. Stick-like legs were wrapped in tight black jeans, ripped across the thighs and calves, and through the frayed tears she could see more black fishnet criss-crossing his pale skin; Reece was always wearing hosiery, for fashion purposes and to indulge his own kinks.

Maisy flashed him a quick smile and finished up serving an attractive woman, bagging her lingerie purchases. "Have a pleasant evening."

The look the woman gave her was one that suggested 'pleasant' was not strong enough a word to describe the mischief she intended for tonight. "And you."

Maisy ushered her to the door and Reece held it open for the woman, who thanked him and disappeared into the darkening evening.

"Hi, sexy," Reece said to Maisy as she hurried past him to the door. She poked her head out into the cold evening air, glancing up and down the street to ensure there were no potential customers approaching. Satisfied, she pulled the door closed, locked it, yanked down the blind and flicked off the neon 'open' light. Reece pretended to be offended. "You not speaking to me?"

She clutched him by the wrist, his spike-studded gauntlet digging into her palm, and she pushed him back against the door and was on her knees and unbuttoning his jeans. "I'm so horny I think I'm going to explode."

"Don't let me stop you," he said, and she tugged his trousers down to ruffle around his boots, exposing the black fishnet holdups he was wearing. It turned her on to see him in hosiery; she loved guys who were willing to experiment, and Reece was like a pioneer in the field. She tugged down his tight boxers and his seven inches of white meat was already primed and stiff for her; Reece never let anyone down when they needed a hard tool.

Maisy sucked saliva into her mouth and lashed her tongue across the underside of Reece's cock before taking the fat head into her mouth and plunging it to the back of her throat. Years of practice had reduced her gag reflex to minimum and all of her conquests were left with incredible stories of her deepthroating expertise. Her hands had yet to touch him, focusing on herself. One hand pinched at her nipples through her flimsy vest, tugging at the silver ring piercings, each pull a barb of pain and pleasure; the other unclasped her jeans and vanished from view, foraging into her panties, wet again with lust, and sought the moist folds of her sex. She zeroed in on her clitoris and worked it harshly, subtlety and care the last thing on her mind, washed away by the desperate need for orgasm.

Reece's hands were in her hair now, balling to take a handful and used it to lever her head even deeper on to him. He brought her lips right to the shaven root of his dick and held her there, savouring every muffled moan. He knew her limits and threshold for holding her breath now and drew her off him at the perfect second. She sucked down air as hungrily as she had taken his lance, never wavering from her own ministrations. Her eyes sparkled behind a film of strained tears and a bead of black mascara ran down her cheek.

He bent and kissed her hungrily, a passionate, wet clinch, licking each other's tongues. He knocked her hand away from her breasts and moved his own across tattooed flesh to grip her tightly, fingers seeking her erect nipple and the steel ring. He rolled them between thumb and forefinger, squeezing to make her suck air through clenched teeth.

"Fuck me," she said. "Make me fucking come."

He pulled her to her feet and resumed their kiss, his hand delving into her panties and coating two fingers with her hot, clammy musk and bringing the digits into their clinch so they both tasted her heat and that deliciously tangy fluid. He turned her away from him and rolled her jeans down to her knees, limiting her movement, placing her at his mercy. She knew to bend over, ass ready for him, and no sooner was the sticky gusset of her panties wrenched aside did he split her eager wet pussy with his cock.

She couldn't contain the sonorous cry of pleasure as he buried himself in her, holding himself there long enough to hook her arms with his. She was trapped in his embrace, impaled upon him; she couldn't move save for an awkward waddle, but she had no intentions to escape. They were interlocked as they had been so many times before; not slaves to such a limiting thing as a steady relationship, but fuck buddies, explorers of desire and kink. He was standing perfectly still now, and she could feel his teasing smile.

"Don't tease me, asshole, I'm not in the mood. Fuck me."

"Oh, aren't we cranky tonight?" he chuckled, and she bucked back against him; if he wasn't going to play, she'd use him. Her aggression was all he needed, and he thrust into her with long, quick motions.

"Oh fuck, that's it, keep that up you bastard," she panted, finally on her way to the climax the day had denied her. She squeezed her thighs together to put more tension on the cock reaming within. "Pull my fucking hair."

Reece didn't need to be told twice, keeping one of her arms wrenched back and clutching her hair, arching her back. She belonged to him now, her toy, a willing hole to be used and satisfied. She felt incredible, her whole body alive with fizzing static, a burning tightness focused at her nethers. The emo boy in his fishnet holdups and the tattooed punk princess fucked like the world was about to end, with total disregard for propriety or romance. It was swift and intense and neither wanted it to end.

Maisy shuddered and shrieked as the orgasm she had craved for hours finally dawned, shattering her into pieces. She bucked and flopped with each wave of pleasure but Reece wouldn't let her go until he was done. With a squeeze of her forearm that would leave a handprint for several hours and a final pull of her hair, he grunted his own climax and flooded her. They collapsed then, orgasms still blazing, still entwined. Two sets of knees hit the bare floorboards hard but the pain only added to the pleasure. Reece's body pushed Maisy's to the deck, holding her flat as he burrowed his face into her neck, biting softly. They breathed in unison as he pumped his last drop into her.

"Oh fuck, I needed that," she cooed softly.

Wordlessly he withdrew, holstering his spent weapon and pulling up his jeans. He helped her to her feet and she did the same, letting his seed spill into her panties; she'd feel used and slutty until she changed and it would be wonderful.

With barely a word spoken she floated through the final lock up procedure, finalising the day's tally, bring down the remote-shutters and ensuring all the lights were off. They floated out into the night like air, appetites already building for more fun.

NYLON
A Poem

A treat with a gossamer glaze,
Ready to be consumed;
Your legs, in liquid silk, are
A gift you grant me to unwrap.
But I shall forever leave them
Sealed within that sheen.
I crave the hiss of my flesh against the fibre,
The cool, slick razing of bare calves on yours.
Tantalising and tactile,
Sensation and searing lust.
I will trace every seam
With fingertip and tongue.
I will follow every thread
Of your delightful second skin,
As I worship the one beneath,
With a passion that will
Never ladder or tear.

MILE HIGH NYLONS

As the private jet reached cruising altitude, Steve finally allowed himself to relax; regardless of how regularly he flew, take-off and landing always made him nervous. Admittedly, the luxuriant surroundings of this chartered plane tempered his anxiety a little; it barely shuddered as it lifted off the ground, slicing through the air with the precision of a craft designed meticulously for comfort and speed, and the plush seat on which he sat hugged his body without the need for the belt.

Ms. Thorpe was indeed a woman of refined taste.

One had only to look at the quality of her product, at the range and success of the company Steve's advertising firm was about to get into bed with to promote their newest line, to see the kind of superiority that Miranda Thorpe created as standard. He was being flown in style across country to meet tomorrow with Ms. Thorpe, to pitch a portfolio of ideas for marketing her new lingerie line; the meeting would make or break the contract between the two firms, and he hoped to high heaven that his proposed campaign would satisfy her. From a professional standpoint it meant an influx of cash from one of the most lucrative companies on the planet; from a personal view, to spend six months shooting with models in the kind of sensual clothing that *Liquid Velvet* made would be a dream come true.

When the plane levelled out he finally began to relax, but nothing could prepare him for the soothing effect of Ms. Thorpe's dedicated in-flight team. When boarding he had met only one of them, but now they were a trio, a heavenly band of sky maidens here to serve his needs. They emerged from the curtain at the front of the cabin, walking in practised, elegant unison on legs that seemed never to end, slender yet strong, encased perfectly in black seamed holdups, the band of which peeked from beneath the hem of their uniforms. Each wore matching black heels and velvet gloves, and upon their heads was perched a hat like a cherry atop a delectable treat. Ms. Thorpe had selected them to appeal to any follicular pigment preference he may have: Helena's blonde bob hung at her jaw, contrasting against full, blood-red lips; Violet's raven tresses cascaded in curls down her back; and Juliette wore her silky auburn hair in a coiling plat that draped over her shoulder, the vibrant red hair in contrast to her freckled complexion. Were he to be honest, he had always preferred blondes, but he certainly was not going to quibble or hurt anybody's feelings. Each of them was a vision of feminine perfection, chosen as the cabin crew for male passengers to put them at total ease, though the swell of indecent thoughts that roiled in Steve's mind were not doing much to leave him composed.

"How are you feeling now, Mr. Johnson?" Helena asked, striding behind his free standing chair and sliding nimble fingers against his tailored suit, showing a surprising amount of strength as she kneaded the tension from his shoulders; today had been a day of meetings, last minute checks and preparations, and with tomorrow's big meet hanging over him it had not been conducive to relaxation. These ladies were to take care of that. He moaned involuntarily at her deft ministrations, feeling his muscles relax. The stresses of the day and the prospect of tomorrow began to evaporate.

"Much better, Helena, thank you. But you girls really don't need to – "

"You're relaxation is our goal, Mr Johnson. Ms. Thorpe wants you to have the finest flight possible and the best night before your meeting tomorrow. She takes care of her clients."

On cue, Violet produced an ice bucket with a full bottle of champagne and Juliette conjured a glass as if from nowhere, and he watched the bubbling liquid fill the flute to the brim, a small frothing drop spilling onto the redhead's hand. With an innocent smile she ran her tongue against the cream to keep it from falling to the floor. She handed him the glass. "Enjoy."

He sipped at it, the act of taking in the delicious beverage easing him before even a single bit of alcohol entered his system. He took in every inch of the girls before him, their slender beauty and those legs, wrapped in the finest black nylon, seams running across calves and thighs and vanishing just beneath the hem of their skirts.

Getting this account was such a desire because it would bring him into contact with girls like this every day. He didn't care how hot-bloodedly male or chauvinistic that made him sound; he was the perfect gentleman when the situation called for it, but like any straight man he adored feminine beauty.

Soft, rhythmic and wordless music drifted through the cabin from hidden speakers, and as Helena worked the stresses from his shoulders and neck her colleagues began to sway in time to the beat, hips rolling, bodies coming into contact as if they were slow dancing in a nightclub to arouse onlookers; it was certainly working. He shifted uncomfortably, still too self aware. Helena's hot breath and soft voice kindly tickled his ear.

"Relax," she insisted. "This is all for you. Everything that's coming."

Her hands slipped around his neck and sank to his throat, deftly unbuttoning it the top of his shirt, those cool fingers vanishing beneath the silk, nails gently raking the hard flesh of his pectorals. Violet and Juliette ground against one another with more fervour now; the brunette clutched the redhead's buttocks and Juliette responded by lifting her leg, her skirt rolling back across her thigh to fully reveal the complex stitching of her holdup band as her leg hooked around Violet's waist.

Steve tried to fathom the situation. Were they air hostesses who doubled as lapdancers, or perhaps even escorts? Or merely the latter playing a role? It was futile to imagine, and would wreck the illusion. *Surrender to it,* Steve thought, testosterone and arousal blotting out any sense of propriety or logic. *If Ms. Thorpe has laid on this treat, it would be rude to turn it down.*

Violet held Juliette firmly as she arched backwards, leg still hooked against the brunette's thigh, holding her in place as she bent with a gymnast's flexibility. Her platted hair snaked against the floor and gravity snatched the hat from her head. Showing off her core, she whipped back to standing, giggling at her own skill, and as if with pride Violet's garnet lips brushed against those of her agile friend. Glistening lips parted to allow their tongues to forage, meeting hungrily, both of them quickly flushing with passionate energy.

Helena's breath was hot against his neck and her lips closed against his, kissing the finely shaven area as she scratched his chest, the rasping sensation of nails against gym-sculpted musculature and waxed flesh coupling with the two-girl show before him to bring the tension back, but this time it was all below the waist.

The dancing girls were quick to notice and broke their clinch, striding to either side of his chair and, in perfect synchronicity, raising their outer legs and perching them on the armrests, giving him a close up view of their legs, wrapped so succulently in expensive nylon, the height of their six inch black heels drawing out the tautness of their calves which he so desperately desired to touch. He reached gingerly for them, and the ladies made no attempt to move. The pads of his fingers caused that marvellous friction of flesh against nylon, and they traced the seams up across the crooks of two delicate knees. He grew bolder, squeezing the flesh of the underside of their raised thighs, hands drifting closer to the goal of their nethers, both hidden beneath dark, flimsy panties.

He loved the look of a lady in hosiery of any sort, and the *feel* of nylon was like heaven to him. For him it was the very definition of femininity; a women accentuating her natural beauty with decorative and sensual clothing, heightening the pleasures of the flesh with intricately crafted garments and creating a perfect visual and tactile experience.

Tactile was the word that brought him from his revelry as the statuesque vixens pivoted at their narrow waists and clutched at the bulge in his crotch, sharing the duties evenly to unveil his hidden weapon; Violet unclasped the belt and slid it fluidly from the trouser loops, while Juliette popped the button and unzipped.

They exposed his expensive white underwear and gently raked perfectly manicured nails across the swell of his lust, eliciting a seething rasp from between gritted teeth. The brunette worked her fingertips beneath the elastic of his briefs and eased it slowly downward to unveil his hard manhood, seven and a half sturdy inches being invited to heaven. With an approving smile, redheaded Juliette gripped it by the well-shaven root and stroked it with devotion, allowing Violet to work the head between thumb and forefinger.

Steve's last shred of propriety evaporated as he ran his hands across the girls nylon-coated calves as they ran theirs over his erection. From behind him, Helena unbuttoned his shirt all the way down, scraping nails against defined abdominal muscles, encouraging her friends to do the same with their free hands. As they took over,

Helena came around and lowered to her knees between his legs, her lipstick glistening, her eyes hungry and full of promise.

"Relax, Mr Johnson," she winked.

Helena's tongue slid against the underside of the head of his cock without need for an invitation. Surrendering to the situation completely he welcomed her advances; for a second he threw his head back as she sank his length into the moist warmth of her mouth, but he did not want to miss a sumptuous visual second of this, locking his eyes on to the scene before him; in his more fantastical imaginings he had fantasised about this kind of situation, of being attended to by more than one woman, but those thoughts were usually reserved for fiction and pornography. Not today.

He caressed the raised thighs of Helena's colleagues for as long as they would allow, but they had other plans, lowering to their knees beside the blonde and assisting her expert ministrations, leaning in to flick each side of his shaft with deft tongues. Helena angled his glistening cock to each side one by one, allowing Violet and Juliette to take him fully into their mouths, heads bobbing on slender necks, making satisfying moans as they tasted his flesh and the early signs of his joy, seeping from his bulbous head.

Helena, ever the woman in charge, ordered the girls to continue and stood, turning her back to Steve, legs apart, her incredible calves and thighs like solid steel.

"Unzip me," she told him, and he didn't hesitate, slowly pulling open the pink uniform from the nape of her neck all the way to the base of her spine, exposing white skin and the clasp of an expensive and intricately designed *Liquid Velvet* bra. With an imperceptible shrug, Helena cast off the uniform; it formed a silky puddle around her black heels, leaving her open to the elements in naught but her shoes, seamed holdups, black lace panties and bra, those black velvet gloves, and the dainty hat of her uniform.

Helena turned, revealing the maximised cleavage of her small but perfectly round breasts, and she pivoted with feminine fluidity to bring them to his face; she clutched his hair determinedly, inviting deeper nuzzling, smiling at the feel of his warm breath on her flesh. A strange sensation filled him; that of falling, of drifting gradually through space, but the plane had lost no altitude, encountered no turbulence. When finally she drew away, he realised he had been negotiated into an almost horizontal position, Helena's fingers discreetly working the seat-tilt controls while playfully smothering him.

The two angels giving his saliva-slickened cock such devotion left it untended as they unzipped each other, slipping out of their shiny uniforms until they were in an identical state of dress to their boss. He lay there feeling like a king in an ancient land surveying his harem, but he knew deep down that they were the ones with true power in this situation, allowing him to believe he was in charge, but he was their willing slave.

"Lie back and enjoy the ride, Mr Johnson," Helena insisted, and with a graceful, feline motion she swept a leg up and over the head rest to bring him face to face with the finely-woven gusset of her black panties, darkened with tantalising moisture. Without invitation she lowered it to his face and he inhaled her sweet musk as the wetness met his pursed lips. He felt her palms grip the headrest at either side of his head, giving her leverage to grind herself against him. Desperate to get deeper he hooked a finger around the sodden material and pulled it aside, giving himself free access to the delicacies of her nethers, lips warm and wet as he tended to them with his tongue, drawing satisfied moans from Helena's throat. She was delicious, succulent, perfumed and pristine and every lap brought great stiffness to his aching tool. Violet and Juliette would not let it go to waste and sucked ravenously, spitting and massaging and priming him for entry.

Steve's vision was obscured by the white cliff of Violet's stomach, leading up to the beautifully rising mounds of her beasts and an angelic face gazing down upon him, lip bitten in swelling ecstasy. So it was that he had no idea who straddled him and slid his member into her. He felt a pair of gloved hands stabilizing his dick and guiding it through the shallow moist pool as the other sky maiden sank her flimsy weight onto him and began working a slow and firm rhythm. It was a blissful mystery but felt wonderful.

Helena swept her leg away and revealed it was Juliette riding him, her auburn plat hanging across her and nestled between bra-wrapped breasts. She slid her hands beneath his unbuttoned shirt and gripped his muscular shoulders, nails tangible beneath her gloves, burrowing into flesh, seeking purchase. She leaned into kiss him, moaning with giddy delight as she tasted the essence of Helena left upon his lips and tongue. It was almost too much and he had to throw himself out of the moment to maintain his composure lest he empty himself within the redhead's tight grove.

Helena and Violet didn't help matters. They came either side of his chair and raised a leg, planting shiny high heels into the arm rest, bracketing the auburn minx as she ground herself against him. She released his shoulders and hooked her arms around their calves, leveraging her weight, using them as support. He watched his rod plunging into her, coated with her glistening fluid.

His hands went out to steel himself and found only the nylon of Helena and Violet's thighs. The gossamer material stretched like webbing under his clutching grasp, melding thin denier material and hot flesh.

Stay focussed on something else... he told himself, but it was an impossibility.

Salvation came just in time, as did Juliette. Her breathing deepened and she whimpered. Her chest had speckled with red and her beautiful face contorted in a display of joy. She shuddered an elegant climax and slid from Steve a second before he crashed over the point of no return. As cold, soothing air assaulted his slick and swollen cock, Juliette's friends held her aloft, her thighs visibly quivering with the glowing effects of her orgasm.

"I think Mr Johnson needs a time out," Violet noted, running a gloved finger through the beaded sweat on his forehead then pushing the moist pad to her tongue.

"A quick lapse, ladies. I don't want to pass the blame, but you're all rather arousing."

Floating on her post-climactic cloud, Juliette sprawled onto a couch and began to pleasure herself, splaying her lips once more. Steve wanted to taste the pussy he had just fucked, but he didn't act quickly enough, for Helena's blonde head sank between her parted thighs and her tongue tended to those fleshy folds. Juliette whimpered and giggled in delight.

Violet sat astride Steve's knee, arm around his neck, as casual as if she was a girlfriend watching a movie with him, but the movie was very much real and as wonderfully pornographic as anything he'd ever seen. Helena's haunches were raised, her ass a perfect peach, and with amazing balance she reached back and slid her underwear over the crest of those cheeks and down her thighs. It was an invitation.

Violet took it, but not as Steve expected her to. She extended a slender leg and ran her toes up the seam of Helena's holdups, along the ornate band then between her thighs. The nylon around her big toe brushed through the furrow of Helena's exposed haven. The blonde moaned against Juliette's quim and the redhead arched her back in ecstasy.

With the flexibility of a gymnast, Violet recalled her leg and pivoted it to bring her flexing toes before Steve's face. The transparent nylon had darkened with Helena's essence and he smelled that familiar musk. He couldn't resist it, clutching Violet's ankle and running his tongue across the nylon foot, all the way to the big toe which he sucked at, soaking up the juices from the blonde. Violet wanted some too and leaned in, licking her own toe, their tongues fighting over the remnants of Helena's pussy moisture. Steve gasped as Violet's hand closed around his dick and began to stroke with fervent urgency.

There was no hesitation in him now; he lifted her with ease, brought her spine against his chest and drove his cock into her like a guided missile. She cried out as he sank into her, forcing down on her hips, filling her tight. A hand came up to her throat, holding her steady, twisting her face so he could stare into her deep brown eyes. He let her take control and she roiled against him.

"Oh, Mr Johnson, you're incredible," she breathed and he kissed her cherry-red lips hungrily.

"I'm only as good as the people I work with," he said, and took a handful of her hair, pivoting her forward until she was cheek-to-cheek with Helena's exquisite buttocks. The brunette wasted no time, taking Helena's hips and kissing her rump while Steve thrust within her. Over the crest of her bobbing head he watched Helena dine upon Juliette. The redhead mewled and turned her heels to the roof of her cabin, hypnotising him with the swaying holdup seams set against milky white skin.

"Mmm, tongue my ass," he heard Helena say, and he realised Violet was devouring her most intimate of holes in preparation. "Get it ready for Mr Johnson…"

It quickened him and with no mercy or tenderness he pounded up into Violet as deep as she could take him, and the new found urgency brought a wail of delight from her. Her cunt tightened its grip on him and he steeled himself against it, willing his body to endure, every nerve in him on edge; as wonderful as this was he wanted to take the blonde over that couch, to penetrate her ass.

Violet came for him and he lifted her up, sturdy rod slipping from her, more rigid now than ever. He laid her on the couch at Juliette's feet and took up a position behind Helena, whose hands were splaying her buttocks, bidding him entry to her glistening puckered hole. He stripped off his shirt completely. He couldn't deny himself the pleasure of her and fed the swollen tip of his cock into the collar of her anus; it flexed but maintained a deliciously tight seal around him as he eased it in with mouth-watering resistance. Helena moaned, discomfort and pleasure soon transformed into only the latter. Juliette sat up and flanked her with Violet and they stroked her hair soothingly, whispering encouragement.

"Oh, there's a good girl," Juliette said.

"He's so big," Violet said. "Doesn't he feel wonderful?"

Helena was breathless, panting, chin slick with moisture from Juliette's snatch. "Amazing…"

Steve glided between those cheeks and forgot the world, forgot tomorrow's meeting, forgot that he was on his knees up in the clouds with the servitude of the three sexiest women he'd ever seen. He was merely here, now, in this instant, body primed, fantasies fulfilled, a slave to pleasure.

He withdrew and the two girls whom had already come for him rolled Helena over and held her on the couch by draping their legs across her stomach. Her own legs flexed around him, drawing him in, toes pointing together to form a ring around his body. He slid into her ass once more, a perfect snug fit, watching four nylon-slick legs brushing one another and the perfect skin of Helena's flat belly. A leg would lift, come to his face and he licked the gossamer strands of the black fibre, smelled their perfume and sweat and sweet essence. Toes under whisper-like threads traced across his chest on their return journey. All the while Helena watched him, eyes wide with lust and elation as he respectfully invaded her. She freed her breasts from the cups of her bra, tweaking her nipples with surprising force. He rolled a thumb across the swollen bud of her clitoris, drawing her inexorably near. He was a gentleman, after all, and refused to leave her unsatisfied.

Her climax came, starting as a deep, ululating cry in the pit of her throat and finally thundering through the cabin as every muscle in her lithe form clenched and convulsed. Her skin shimmered with sweat and her gloved hands closed around the calves of her colleagues, holding on as her consciousness dismantled and reformed before their eyes.

Seeing her pleasure spill out with such vociferous strength was Steve's final trigger. He could wait no longer but could not pass up the opportunity, sliding free of her squeezing canal and venting across the chaotic array of legs and gloved palms before him. Arcs of creamy fluid spattered their waiting shins and toes, soaking in trails across the denier fabric, stretched into ever expanding paths by velvet-snug fingers. The girls brought droplets of his come to their lips and sucked it deep, all the while rubbing their legs together, melding flesh, textiles and his warm gift together.

Steve collapsed, more satisfied than he had ever been before, across that hot miasma of limbs and nylon. Helena kissed his forehead while Violet and Juliette gently caressed his back and arms. Together they breathed, starved of oxygen at high altitudes, light headed and giddy. He had no clever words for them.

They had taken him apart amongst the clouds like angels, spiriting him off into a new future in their company with a heavenly host, rich with such potential, and he couldn't wait to embrace it.

DRESSED
A Poem

Suited in silk, I stride in
To where you lay in wait.
On shimmering sheets,
Encased in lace.

I see you crave me,
The tell tale signs
Are written upon you,
Like the gossamer threads at your thighs.

The curl of your lips under teeth,
The eyes that iris, hungry for me.
The swell of your breast, and the
Darkening spread of joy betwixt hips.

You want me, you need me,
In your ribbons and bows.
I'll unwrap your desires,
But the clothes will stay on.

Cufflinks glimmer in eyes hungry for me.
Clad in threads tailored for you
To go giddy on sight, woven around me
To stir up your lust.

We dress for the occasion,
Refined and replete in passion.
I'm your gentleman, you're my lady,
We belong here and now.

My tie threads loose
Into hands you fall weak beneath.
They bind your wrists
And our evening begins...

A FRIENDLY RIVALRY

1

It was a competition between them. It always had been.

Kathryn and Shelley had known each other since school, and rivalry had been as common an activity to them as homework and sneaking cigarettes behind the boiler house. Their friendship had weathered petty jealousies, puberty and conflicts over the opposite sex, but the endless one-upmanship had never gone away. It was a game to them, a constant contest of friendly dominance.

To study them on a strictly physical basis was to see opposites; Kathryn was tall and svelte, straight through the hips, long-legged with only the faintest hint of breasts, whereas Shelley barely touched five feet tall and was amply curved in all the places one could desire, with a pair of huge breasts that looked as if they could topple her tiny stature at a moment's notice. Kathryn was pale skinned and fair haired; Shelley's hair jet-black and worn in long curls, her skin a dark brown hue, the product of mixed-race parents. Kathryn had age over Shelley, her birthday falling a full week before her friend; but now that Shelley had turned eighteen two days previous, both were satisfied to be the same age for another year.

It would be another matter, however, that would cause their playful enmity tonight, one that had been the cause so many times before, and one that would continue for as long as they would know each other: boys.

No. They were eighteen now.

Men.

"I bet I can get off with more men than you tonight," Kathryn wagered as they prepared for the evening's celebrations. She was standing in front of her full-length bedroom mirror, still wrapped in her blue robe, straightening her hair. Shelley was sitting at the vanity table behind, clad in a black lace bra and panties, hair already done into her usual thick, curl-accentuating style, applying her eye makeup between sips of wine. Her dark lips left delicate stains on the glass.

"I'll take that bet," she said. "What does the winner get?"

"Pride," Kathryn explained. "And more guys than the other one."

Kathryn finished her hair and dropped the robe, running hands across her slender body, knowing that Shelley had the advantage when it came to breasts and behind; it never affected her chances too harshly, but she would love, for one evening, to have a pair of tits guaranteed to draw more looks. She looked at Shelley's reflection in the mirror as the girl applied mascara, running her eyes over every curve, the huge swell of her breasts and the chasm of cleavage the tight bra gave her. Her skin was perfect, a shade perfectly balanced between ebony and ivory that men loved; they thought she was exotic. Everything about her oozed sexuality.

Kathryn poured herself a glass of wine and turned to her wardrobe to select her final outfit.

Unbeknownst to her, Shelley was looking at her in the reflection of her own table mirror. Shelley knew her body was appealing to men but she hated being so short; she saw the way men looked at Kathryn as soon as she walked into places, towering over others, perfectly thin and elegant. There wasn't a spare ounce of fat on Kathryn, whereas Shelley had to work hard to keep her curves on the right side of chubby. She envied Kathryn's stature, watching now as her friend sat on the bed amidst the mess of already-discarded clothes and reached into a nearby drawer, selecting a pair of balled-up stockings and dipping her pointed toes into them, rolling the fine black material up those perfect, endless legs.

Kathryn pulled on her dress, a short, simple black number with a high neckline that was rimmed with sparkling costume-gems. She turned her back to Shelley.

"Zip me up."

Shelley did so, encasing her friend in the material for the night's festivities. She smacked Kathryn's right ass cheek in mischief.

"You look gorgeous. I'm still going to win though."

"Oh yeah?"

"Oh, *definitely* yeah."

Kathryn sipped her wine as Shelley finished her makeup and put on her own outfit, a figure hugging blue mini-dress that accentuated and exaggerated every plentiful curve, making her look like a petite shrink-wrapped present that any man would be desperate to unwrap. She admired herself in the mirror, pushing her breasts into position, her plunging neckline showing off the gargantuan cleavage.

"We'll see, bitch," Kathryn said, draining the last of her alcohol. "We'll see."

*

The first club they went into was heaving, packed with bodies drinking and dancing, and as they made their way across the threshold, their outfits and attitudes had the desired effect. Men were looking at them, eyeing them up and down, appraising in a way that should have offended and upset them, but it didn't. This was what they wanted: to be stared at, to be worshipped, and to be considered goddesses amongst mortal girls.

Both knew how to achieve power over men, but now that they were women in the eyes of society they had nothing to fear about doing something about it. Not that it had ever stopped them in the past; both had lost their virginities to boys now long out of the picture, and had pursued others in the intervening years and months. They had each notched up a range of sexual partners. Some of the primmer girls at college had called them sluts because they weren't afraid of sex; but why deny themselves something they enjoyed for the sake of propriety?

Still – before hitting the eighteen-year milestone there was always wariness, an exciting danger, but a danger they were thankful had now fallen away, never to be missed. Being a slut before eighteen, while never a real problem, was an emblem you had to bear in the face of mockery and scornful glances from other girls; now, as women, being a slut was a badge of honour.

Being girls was exciting, but they were *women* now, and that was truly thrilling. They could do anything, because the simple fact was, while boys and men will chase and pursue girls, it is *women* that they really want.

They fought their way to the bar, pushing in front of a pair of men in their late twenties, smiling suggestively to deflect any tension.

"What are you girls having?" the taller of the two asked predictably.

"You, hopefully," Shelley told him. "But vodka and coke will do for the time being."

The men bought drinks and they sank them quickly, moving their targets onto the dance floor and grinding against them. The men, whose names they never cared to learn, couldn't believe their luck, least of all when each of the girls tossed each other a wink and moved in on their targets with a kiss.

When they finally pulled away, both of the girls said they needed to visit the ladies room and walked off arm-in-arm; the men fully expected them to return but they never did, exiting the club and moving on to another.

That was how it went, hopping from club to club, using nothing more complicated than a batted eyelash or seductive word to obtain drinks and scores in their game. Sometimes they would abandon a venue after notching up one each; at others they would relocate to another area of the club, a secluded spot or another floor, and continue their tally.

The evening's events altered slightly somewhat when they met Paul and his friend Tom.

Kathryn had shared some classes at college with Paul. He was as tall as she, well built without being too large and handsome enough without being overtly cocky. Though not shy, he was quiet and collected, rarely speaking unless it was necessary. Kathryn had had a crush on him during their time at college together, or at least a desire to let him take her in the common room, but he had always been with his girlfriend, whose name she couldn't now remember. She had been a quiet brunette who never appeared particularly suited to Paul's tastes, but they had been together nonetheless.

Paul was standing with Tom and another girl, though those two barely noticed Paul was there, flirting and giggling and kissing like two drunk fools in love or lust, whichever was most likely to get them laid that night.

"Why are you staring at that bloke?" Shelley asked, looking around for potential targets.

"What's wrong with him?" Kathryn argued.

"Nothing's wrong with him. He's not exactly a stud, though."

"I never found out."

"Look at those two over there by the bar, they're fit," Shelley noted with a nod towards a pair of strangers, but Kathryn had already walked away, heading straight towards Paul. "Oh, right then," Shelley said. "I'll fly solo with this one, shall I?"

Paul saw Kathryn coming and he smiled broadly, genuinely pleased to see her. They hugged.

"Kathryn!" he said, as if to reassure himself that he really *did* remember her name. "How's it going?"

"Ah, you know, not bad."

"You look great," he said, looking her up and down in a manner that had nary a hint of lascivious leer, and she caught his appraising glance and felt lifted.

"Thanks, so do you."

"Guys, this is Kathryn, I went to college with her. This is Tom and Sally."

Tom and Sally greeted her with the kind of curt smiles that are given to someone who is interrupting important business, and went back to kissing.

"Ignore them, they haven't been together long. So what are you doing with yourself?"

"Buy me a drink and I'll tell you all about it."

"Thank you, you've saved me from being the third wheel."

They drank together while Shelley, somewhere across the bar, was busy boosting her tally by two. Kathryn listened to Paul as he told her what he was doing now, but none of the information really sunk in; he was nice, and polite, and gentlemanly, but the crush she had at college had been purely physical, and that hadn't changed. She didn't want to be his friend, or his girlfriend, only his lover, and only once – or potentially a few occasions, if he was good enough to warrant repeat sessions.

"So, you're single, Paul?" she asked.

"At the moment. I broke up with Hannah a few months ago. You remember Hannah from college?"

"Yeah. You were so much better than her."

"I don't know about that," Paul said, wondering why Kathryn had now gripped the collar of his shirt.

"I do," she said, and kissed him without any more preamble. He was nervous, but swiftly relaxed into it, both of them tipsy now, their mouths tinged with the taste of alcohol. It was a passionate and deep embrace, her hands lowering to his waist, fingers curling over the lip of his trousers.

"Come with me," Kathryn said, suddenly overcome.

"Where are we going?"

She led him through the crowd, blowing a quick kiss to Shelley as she danced with a man who was the wrong side of forty; her friend looked back with a look of confusion that soon turned to realisation.

Kathryn led Paul past a bouncer focused on a brewing argument between two young men, and pushed him through the door of the male toilets. There was nobody currently inside and she dragged him into a cubicle in a flurry of anxious breaths, dropping the toilet seat and making him sit.

"Kathryn, this is – " Paul said breathlessly, brimming with nerves.

She dropped her weight into his lap, straddling him, feeling the bulge in his pants grow against her.

"Paul, this is simple. Either you want this or you don't. Do you want this?"

"Well, yes, but – "

"Then shut your mouth."

He was taken aback by her bluntness. "I'm just not used to – "

She unbuckled his belt and plunged her hand into his trousers, straight to the strengthening rod within. He breathed harshly in response, his sentence forgotten.

She slid his trousers and shorts down to his knees, releasing his caged member, standing proud, seven inches of sturdy meat awaiting her touch. She denied herself not a second longer, bending at the hip.

Her mouth sank around it, taking it as deep as it would go, almost to the root. Around the remaining band of exposed flesh she gripped and pumped a perfect rhythm with the movement of her mouth. Paul writhed at her technique. Her red lips slid up and down his length, tongue coating his dick with a film of saliva. He could feel something hard amidst the soft flesh of her tongue, and when she ran the tip of her tongue down his shaft he saw the glinting metal orb of her tongue piercing.

Paul's fingers clenched into fists and he gave an uncontrollable grunt.

Kathryn knew too late what that signified, and felt the gush of his hot seed in her mouth, striking the back of her throat and causing her to swallow involuntarily. She pulled away and released the grip on his penis, further spurts of creamy white tonic dripping from his bulbous head and spattering onto his thighs.

"Is that it?" she said, unable and unwilling to hide the disappointment in her voice.

"I'm sorry, I just wasn't expecting that!"

Kathryn wiped a trickle of his leftovers from her lip and smeared it petulantly on his jeans.

"That's never happened to me before," he explained. "I was just *so* turned on."

"Oh, don't give me that," Kathryn said. "It's my fault for being so fucking sexy, is that it?"

"I didn't mean that, I just – "

Kathryn stopped listening to him, morose at a fantasy unfulfilled; the only evidence of the encounter was the salty aftertaste on her tongue.

"You," she said, refusing to let this be the end, "get one more shot at this. I want to fuck you, and that's that. If you've got a bit more warning, surely you can keep control over yourself a bit longer, right?"

"I suppose," he said, standing and zipping up his trousers, trying in vain to wipe the soaked-in mess from the denim. "Give me some time and – "

"Not tonight," she said, pulling out her phone. "I don't want you getting attached, or clingy, or broody. Give me your number and keep tomorrow night free, okay?"

"Uh, okay," he said, and he gave her his phone number. An awkward silence descended that he saw fit to break. "Should we go for a drink?"

"I've drunk enough of what you have to offer tonight, I think," she said, and strutted out, slamming the cubicle door behind her.

2

Kathryn and Shelley fell through the front door and into Kathryn's bedroom, heads still abuzz with the evening's delights. Shelley turned on her speakers, cranked up the music and flicked on the bedside lamp as Kathryn poured the remainders of their pre-night-out bottle of wine into their two lipstick-stained glasses, and they danced together with the wanton abandon of two drunk girlfriends having the time of their lives. When the final burst of adrenaline had worn off they settled onto the bed, kicking off their high heels, drinking their wine and discussing the night's events.

"I think it's safe to say I'm the winner," Shelley said.

"How do you work that out?" Kathryn contested.

"I think thirteen is higher than eleven, don't you?"

"I think what I did in the toilet is worth way more than what you did."

"Nah, a guy's a guy, doesn't matter what you did with him – and I think Mr. Thirty Seconds isn't even worth a full one."

"That was such a gutter," Kathryn said dejectedly. "I've wanted to fuck him since college and he goes and blows it in just a few seconds."

"There's always tomorrow," she argued.

"He'd better be good."

"So, thirteen to eleven. Face it, I'm the winner. I'm just a better catch than you."

"Fuck off," Kathryn laughed. "No chance. They only want you for your tits."

"Here comes the jealousy. I'm a better kisser, too."

"I doubt that very much," Kathryn said, sticking out her tongue, the ball piercing glistening in the lamp light.

Shelley giggled. "You remember when you first got that and I wanted to see what it felt like to kiss someone with a tongue piercing?"

"Of course I remember. That's how I know I'm a better kisser."

"You're off your head," Shelley stated. "Come here, prove it."

"Sounds like a challenge," she said, and eased her head in without any hesitation, their foreheads bumping, noses glancing off one another as their lips met clumsily, jokingly. Their tongues darted out once and struck; Shelley's rolled briefly against the warm metal ball nestled on the bed of tempting moisture that escaped Kathryn's mouth.

"You gay slut," Shelley said. "Straight in there, no messing."

"We should totally do the lesbian thing on a night out, it'll drive the dudes mental. I bet we can pull no problem with a gay routine."

"We can pull no problem without it. You just want to get me into bed, don't you, you naughty lesbian." There was no threat or repulsion in her voice; this was a joke, obviously, two long-time friends laughing about fantasies that would never come to pass. Shelley felt a tickling at the hem of her skirt and looked down to see Kathryn's fingers gently pulling at the material, her thumb idly stroking the flesh above her knee, her red-painted nails clicking at the material of Shelley's stocking. When she looked back to Kathryn's face her pale companion was watching her own dancing fingers with a calm smile, then raised her deep brown eyes to meet Shelley's.

"Stop mucking about!" Shelley giggled with faux-nerves. "Stop giving me that look."

"Why, is it getting you going?"

"You should be so lucky!"

"I know I would," she purred.

Shelley pushed her away now with playful aggression, throwing her thigh over Kathryn's groin and straddling her, the base of Shelley's blue skirt hiking itself up as her legs parted to trap her friend between powerful brown thighs, exposing the perfect curve of her buttocks and her black G-string. Shelley snatched up a pillow and hit Kathryn across the face with playful force.

"You dirty dyke!" she laughed. "I knew it, I always knew it! I bet you've watched me for years. Did you watch me getting ready tonight?" Shelley remembered craftily viewing Kathryn in the mirror, watching her pull on her stockings, and felt a strange buzz to think that Kathryn may have watched her at some point too, admiring her body. "Did you, you slut? Did it get you wet?"

Kathryn wrestled the pillow away and threw it across the room, then quickly snared her by the wrists with her thin but powerful arms. Shelley struggled then fell still, looking down at her friend.

"I'm no lesbian," Kathryn assured her. "I like guys too much. But is there anything wrong with being a little curious?"

Shelley thought, dark eyes glowing with mischievous, seductive interest. "I suppose not."

"You're so beautiful," Kathryn said earnestly. "I wish I looked like you."

"Don't be silly," Shelley responded. "You're a stunner. You know you are. The blokes love you, you're tall and skinny. I'd swap places with you any day."

"I think we can both agree that we think each other is gorgeous."

Shelley shifted her weight slightly, and through the thinness of her dress, Kathryn could feel the warmth radiating from Shelley's crotch, heating a small patch of her stomach. Her skirt was pulled just low enough that she could see nothing between her legs, but knew that only a fine strip of black material covered Shelley's most intimate of areas. The idea of touching it sent a shiver through her.

Kathryn smiled, the thought still lingering. "How drunk are *we*?"

She had relaxed her arms and Shelley pushed them gently back to the bed on either side of Kathryn's head, pinning them in place. She angled her upper body forward and the huge mounds of her breasts promised to spill free from her bra, flesh quivering as she spoke.

"Drunk enough."

Kathryn could smell the sweetness of her breath, tinged with vodka and wine. Shelley's head came in closer still, and Kathryn expected her to laugh and leap away at any moment, but she remained in position. Their eyes met now, dark and darker brown locking together as they moved too close to focus.

They kissed.

This was not a faux kiss the way their first had been, but a genuine gesture. Kathryn had no control of her back as it arched off the bed, forcing her chest up against Shelley's, feeling the roundness of her friend's breasts against her own smaller bosom. Shelley's hands were confidently holding hers in place with serious force, but Kathryn had no desire to escape as their lips pushed together.

Shelley's pink tongue emerged from ruby softness and Kathryn permitted it to glide between her own, opening her mouth to return the motion, her tongue's inquiry light at first then more fervent, matched with equal passion by Shelley's. Wet flesh rolled against its opposite, and Shelley truly felt the small steel ball against her tongue now, bringing back memories of the first time they had kissed as younger girls, the thrilling danger they had both felt at doing something so naughty.

Their saliva mixed and both of them tasted each man the other had kissed earlier in the evening; Shelley even imagined that she could still detect the bitter salt aftertaste of Paul's seed, feeling a great thrill at the prospect of swallowing the tiny traces of him that he had left just a few hours ago.

Finally they broke their clinch and held each other's gaze. Kathryn's cheeks were flushed red, and Shelley's had darkened slightly. They breathed shallowly.

"Who's the better kisser, then?" Shelley smiled.

"Who gives a fuck?" Kathryn said. "We're both pretty damn good." Shelley released her with a chuckle and Kathryn lifted her head off the bed, nuzzling her face into the perfume scented black curls that fell down past Shelley's neck. Their cheeks brushed together as Kathryn's lips found Shelley's ear, nipping at her lobe very gently.

Then she said: "Let me fuck you."

Shelley laughed again, then lowered her head to whisper into Kathryn's ear. "You dirty lesbian, I thought you'd never ask."

Kathryn wasn't giggling now, her mind set on other things as her hands slid down Shelley's back to the meat of her butt-cheeks, those ample, perfect mounds tight under her skirt. Kathryn squeezed the flesh and pulled Shelley closer to her as their lips met again, tongues churning with hunger. Her fingers peeled back the hem of Shelley's skirt so it bunched around her waist, her ass exposed to the air, and Kathryn traced a probing finger down the warm canyon, tickling her anus before reaching the hotbed she aimed for.

Shelley was shaved down below, but the sensitive pad of Kathryn's finger could feel the last remains of stubble around her sex, rasping against it as she snaked a finger around the fine material of her G-string and pulled it aside, allowing fingers to mould against her form.

Shelley gasped as Kathryn's hand cupped her.

"How dare you call *me* a lesbian," Kathryn said. "You're soaking."

Shelley was, her lips already swollen with delight; when Kathryn moved her hand to slide it between their stomachs for better access, a fine sheen of moisture imprinted onto the neck of her stockings. Shelley ground against her, warm and wet and eager.

The taller girl applied pressure, using two fingers to part Shelley's lips with a careful tenderness, and the pad of her thumb to tease the area where those lips came together at the top, bringing her clitoris out to play. Shelley whimpered with enjoyment, immediately on the way to satisfaction, loving that Kathryn had as much of an understanding of the female body as she did; sometimes men could take so long to get going, to find the right spot, but this girl knew her way round like an expert.

Kathryn sank her middle finger into the pink, wet flesh of Shelley's cleft; a harsh breath escaped Shelley's mouth and filled Kathryn's lungs. She worked her finger kindly, her thumb still doing its delicate work, massaging Shelley's walls with a pulsing rhythm. Shelley's hips writhed gently against the touch. One hand reached up and levered against the headboard, the other running through Kathryn's hair, splayed on the pillow, balling to a fist to pull it tight as she approached climax.

"I'm coming," she whispered.

"I can tell," Kathryn smiled.

Shelley let out a tiny yelp and gritted her teeth, legs trembling as Kathryn's fingers brought her to ecstasy. Her sweat-beaded forehead fell against Kathryn's flat chest, and she allowed herself a moment of quiet abandon, losing herself in post-coital warmth.

She heard a sucking sound and angled her head to see Kathryn with her moist fingers in her mouth, tasting Shelley's joy. Her eyes sparkled with delight and anticipation.

Shelley pulled her friend up off the bed and kissed her, fingers only just escaping from her mouth, tasting a mix of herself and Kathryn's saliva. Her hand went to the zipper at the back of Kathryn's dress and worked it quickly; Kathryn stood up on the mattress and let the outfit fall away, standing before her friend, stick-thin and pale, in her bra, panties and stockings.

Kathryn felt a little self-conscious as Shelley eyed her up and down, taking in every inch of her, every tiny goosebump that now rose across her body.

"You get naked, too," she pleaded.

"Not yet."

Still on her knees, Shelley put a firm hand to Kathryn's perfectly flat stomach and pushed her until her back was against the wall; she shivered at the coldness of the surface, then shivered at Shelley's touch. Her friend's hands ran over her narrow hips and down her thighs, to her calves, then came to the inside of her legs and back up.

Shelley peeled aside Kathryn's underwear to reveal a tiny sliver of sculpted pubic hair leading down to pink lips, already glistening.

She slid a finger straight in, moderate but unyielding at the same time, and Kathryn cried out as it entered her all the way to the knuckle. When she tried to move, Shelley's palm forced her back against the wall.

She opened her stocking-clad legs wider to allow Shelley closer, and a second ebony finger found its way inside, working in tandem with the first; Shelley's two digits made a rhythmic beckoning gesture, coaxing Kathryn closer to orgasm, soon caressing her G-spot which brought her to an instant, shuddering and vocal finish.

Giving Kathryn no time to recover, Shelley slid her wet fingers away and closed her mouth around her.

Kathryn cried out again as she felt Shelley's tongue at work against her, gliding over lips and thrusting into her shallow wetness. Her lips pursed around Kathryn's clit and sucked, making her moan and giggle and compose every other sound between.

Kathryn threw her legs over Shelley's shoulders so it was only her friend's strength that kept her in position; her thighs were holding Shelley's head in place too, a captive whom she would allow to dine forever as long as it continued to be this good.

When Kathryn came again she pushed herself off the wall and they fell back to the bed, Shelley's head still between Kathryn's stocking-bound thighs. They laughed as Kathryn quickly dismounted and rolled Shelley over, working the zip of her dress and peeling her from it like ripe fruit from its skin, tossing the garment aside.

The girls kneeled before one another on the bed. Shelley reached back and unclasped her bra, finally unleashing her huge breasts, black nipples pert with excitement.

"I love your tits," Kathryn said, pushing them gently together, sinking her head into the cleavage. Shelley took the opportunity to unhook Kathryn's bra and let out her own tiny breasts, brown nipples perky and alert.

"Yours are so cute," Shelley assured her.

Kathryn's mouth had moved lower now, tongue flicking against a pert black nipple, bringing a smile to Shelley's beautiful face. Shelley cupped both breasts and fed them to her friend, watching each flick of the tongue leave a delicate strand of saliva between nipple and mouth.

"Play with my pussy," Shelley instructed.

Kathryn's fingers went to Shelley's sex and snaked against the gusset of her G-string.

"Get this fucking thing off."

Shelley writhed out of it so that she was completely naked, allowing Kathryn full access to her. Her fingers danced delicately against her lips and clit, making her voluptuous chest heave against Kathryn's face.

"Now play with *your* pussy too," Shelley ordered.

Kathryn slipped her way out of her own panties without ever taking her mouth from Shelley's tits, sucking eagerly as she worked her hands across two sets of pussy lips, bringing pleasure to both. She played with herself the way she always did and demonstrated the same technique on her friend, who seemed to enjoy it just as much as Kathryn did when alone.

Shelley gently pulled at Kathryn's hair and brought their faces together for another kiss. Kathryn's wet fingers left tiny patches on Shelley's shoulder blades as she pulled her closer; Shelley's hands cupped Kathryn's tight ass and moved it nearer.

Their legs scissored together, interlocking, the heat and warmth of their precipice-perched sexes finally touching, kissing, merging into one. The hardened buds of two clits rubbed against each other. Their hips ground in unison, gentle only for a brief spell then fervent and forceful, grinding with an eager passion that brought both to the edge of bliss.

Both of them came in perfect unison, a riotous harmony that left them both momentarily unaware of anything but their joining; surroundings vanished, leaving only hot flesh and contentment. Their breathing synchronised, each resting a head on the other's shoulders, limbs coiled lotus-like together.

As their senses returned they lay down together and kissed tenderly like old lovers, their tongues retired, until both of them fell into comfortable sleep.

*

When morning came nothing was said about their encounter, but likewise there was no embarrassment about what had happened; it was as if the experience had always been expected, waiting just around the corner, and now that it had been had, it was as if the air had been cleared for them to move on as normal.

They dressed and went into town; Kathryn wanted to buy something new for the evening, some lingerie for her as-yet-unorganised session with Paul.

"Are you sure giving him something frilly and sexy to look at won't set him off too early?" Shelley teased as they browsed the racks, admiring a range of bra and panty sets, corsets and teddies.

"To be fair to the guy, I caught him off guard. One minute he was having a drink with his friends, the next he's getting a blowjob in a club toilet. If I was a guy, I think *I'd* have gone off early, too."

"I'd love to be a bloke for a day," Shelley confided, loud enough for a passing older woman to give her a strange look. "Just to see what it's like to fuck someone with a dick."

"You've fucked loads of people with a dick," Kathryn quipped.

"*Using* a dick," she corrected, and her eyes lit up. "We should get a strap-on." It was the first mention of their late-night rendezvous since their mutual orgasm, and Kathryn was surprised to find how normal she felt. The nearby woman made a scoffing sound and gave a withering look that said 'girls these days,' and padded away.

"So you'll keep out of the way tonight?" Kathryn enquired.

"If I have to. What time's he coming – bearing in mind he'll probably get there ten minutes too soon."

"You're hilarious." Kathryn fished into her handbag and took out her phone, making a call to Paul. After a single ring he picked up. "Someone's eager."

"Not too eager, I hope," Shelley said pointedly, and Kathryn gave her a middle finger.

"Hi, yeah," Paul's voice said down the line. "Look, there might be a problem tonight."

"A problem?" Kathryn repeated, and Shelley's interest intensified. "What kind of problem?"

"A Tom kind of problem," Paul explained. "He's – well, he's just broken up with Sally. Well, they've just made it official, they broke up last night."

"And they seemed so enamoured with each other," Kathryn said bracingly. "Couldn't leave each other alone."

"Well, it turns out she can't leave anybody alone. She disappeared a while and he found her getting off with someone she used to go to college with."

"It seems there's a lot of that about."

"He's in a bit of a funk," Paul said. "I don't really want to leave him alone tonight. He needs a shoulder to cry on, a show of male solidarity."

"How about you show us that male solidarity?" Kathryn looked at Shelley, whose attention had wandered now to a rack of white teddies, all frills, fishnet and lace. "Psst."

Shelley came over. Kathryn covered the mouthpiece of the phone and whispered quickly. "How would you like to not have to hide tonight?"

"From lesbian experimentation to a threesome. You're a dark horse."

"He can bring his friend, he was there last night."

Shelley cast her mind back. "He wasn't bad," she shrugged.

"Ask Tom," Kathryn said into the phone, "If he'd rather have a little fun tonight than sit and mope. I've got a friend who'd like to be introduced."

"Hold on," Paul said, and there was a muffled silence as he evidently asked the question to his nearby companion. "Hello? He said okay."

"No need for him to get *too* enthusiastic," Kathryn said sternly.

"Yeah, I'm not as tolerant about premature – " Shelley started, but Kathryn shoved her out of earshot.

"Excellent," Kathryn said. "Nine o'clock tonight." She gave him the address. "We'll make a night of it."

Before he could say anything, she hung up, and turned to Shelley.

"Looks like we're shopping for two."

3

Paul and Tom were a few minutes late. Shelley quipped it boded well for the evening, just before Kathryn opened the door and welcomed them in. Both of them were dressed in shirts and neat trousers, smelled of alluring aftershave and carried a bottle of wine each.

"Evening ladies," Tom said brightly, clearly already riding the moderate buzz of a dose of Dutch courage. Shelley shook his hand and accepted a kiss on the cheek as she took the wine. "Nice to meet you. You look beautiful."

Shelley was wearing a long black gown that hung at her ankles and pulled her waist in tight, exaggerating her breasts and bottom to statuesque proportions.

"So do you," Paul told Kathryn, who was wearing a short black skirt and red silk blouse.

The women thanked them and shared a look; they were not going to be wearing these clothes for much longer, but appreciated the compliment all the same.

They made their introductions and came through to the living room, spotless and lit with lamps rather than the overhead lighting, giving it a muted, homely feel. Music played from the stereo. The girls poured the wine and said very little, letting the nerves of their callers do the talking.

"This is a nice place," Paul said.

"It's a two-bedroom student flat," Shelley said. "It's hardly the Hilton."

They drank deeply of their glasses and the girls relished in how uncomfortable both of the men looked to be; Paul had known what the invite to this place had meant, and whatever he had explained to Tom, the notion hadn't quite settled with either of them.

"So, have you lived here – "

"I don't like small talk and this is fucking miniscule," Shelley stated. "If you'll excuse us just a moment, we'll go and slip into something a little more see-through."

Kathryn and Shelley strode from the room, trying to hold in their laughs; they waited for the door to close and pressed their ears against the wood, listening to the ensuing conversation.

"This is bizarre," Paul said. "We're man-whores!"

"We're not man-whores," Tom argued.

"We're prostitutes that aren't even getting paid!"

"You're such a girl, Paul. We're being offered sex on a plate and you're worried about the ethics of it."

"I'm not, I'm just a bit – I don't want to be listening to you going at it in the next room."

The girls tiptoed into Kathryn's bedroom, eyeing up the lingerie they had bought, already laid out on the bed.

"So, you're sure about this?" Shelley said.

"Why, aren't you?"

"I can't *wait*," she said. "You heard the man. He doesn't want to have to hear his friend through the wall. If everyone's in the same room, there's no risk of that. Unzip me."

She turned from Kathryn and lifted the tendrils of hair up and away from her shoulders, letting her friend ease her zip down. She stepped out of the dress completely and eased into the white corset she had bought earlier, so pure and white that it made her skin seem even darker and more exotic in contrast. The white fishnet holdups she pulled on only exaggerated the effect.

"Come on then, admit it – you want to fuck me again."

"Hold me back," Kathryn said, dressing herself, rolling on a black corset that barely covered her breasts but gave her a little support, emphasising a small cleavage. She stepped into a thong and Shelley slid it up and over her creamy thighs, planting a delicate kiss on her hip. Finally, Kathryn pulled on a pair of sheer black holdups.

They stood next to each other and surveyed their reflection in the mirror, Kathryn's arm draped over Shelley's shoulder, Shelley's arm snaked around Kathryn's hips.

"Those are two lucky young men out there," Shelley said.

"Come on girl, let's give them what for."

They marched into the living room with a perfect stride, and the men immediately ceased whatever conversation they had been having, completely unsure of what to say, or do.

Then the show began.

Shelley and Kathryn kissed, no awkwardness between them now since their tryst last night. Paul and Tom watched as they brushed each other's hair away to grant them a better view, caressing their cheeks and neck gently as their delicate lips brushed together. Then their tongues were involved, living pink creatures wet with saliva, dancing and fighting in the shared area of their mouths.

Paul and Tom shared a look then returned their attention to the girls, undulating together as the music played. The girls pressed opposite cheeks together and fixed their audience in a seductive gaze.

"Do you like that, boys?" Shelley asked.

"Yeah," Tom managed.

"What do you want us to do now?" Kathryn asked.

After some hesitation, Tom's statement sounded like a question. "Play with each other's tits?"

Kathryn leaned forward, placing her face into Shelley's cleavage, and the shorter girl jiggled her breasts back and forth, making a quiet slapping noise against Kathryn's cheeks. Kathryn held them firmly then, teasing her black nipples out of their white holdings and running a quivering tongue over them, drawing a tiny giggle from Shelley.

Shelley now kissed Kathryn's flatter chest, her nipples dark and erect, and she sucked on those petite buds with fervour, holding Tom in her gaze as she did so. "Is this what you like?"

Tom nodded, unable to believe his luck.

"Show me that you like it. I want to see your dick."

Tom looked at Paul nervously.

"What's wrong?" Shelley asked.

"You want to see it – here?"

"Unless you'd rather go out into the street and do it?"

"No, I mean, shouldn't we go into your room? I thought that's why we were here."

Shelley grinned. "We did think about the one-room each thing. But then we thought this was far more fun. And if one of you were to finish a little prematurely, shall we say – naming no names of course…" Paul looked at Kathryn then dropped his gaze. "Then at least we've still got someone to play with."

Paul and Tom looked at each other for a long time, silently deciding whether or not this was something they wanted to be part of, their friendship having weathered plenty, but never before a situation where they would be naked, aroused and having sex in front of one another.

"I'm okay with it if you are," Paul said, not seeming entirely convinced.

Tom let out a slow breath and shrugged. "Okay."

"Excellent," Shelley smiled. "So come on then, Tom, get your dick out for the girls."

Tom unbuckled his belt nervously and folded the flaps of his trousers back to expose the bulge in his shorts, which looked to have diminished somewhat during their discussion. He glanced at Paul, who was looking away now, anywhere else but at his friend's tool.

"Come on," Shelley said. "This is a once in a lifetime opportunity, a four-way with two beautiful girls. We can always get dressed and watch TV if you'd prefer."

"For fuck's sake," Tom said, and pulled his shorts down, exposing his shriveling member. It was a good length, Shelley noted, but shaming him hadn't helped.

"That's better," she said. "I think that's enough embarrassment for one day, too."

She padded over to him and settled down on the couch, straddling a knee, one hand going to the back of his head and pulling his mouth to her chest, suckling him at her dark teats, her other hand gently cradling his tightening testicles as his shaft responded positively again.

Kathryn looked at Paul, who still looked more than a little uncomfortable. "I know this wasn't quite the plan but it shouldn't change anything. So come on. Your turn now."

Paul slid himself out of his trousers and pants completely, letting his member stretch to its full, powerful length as Kathryn lowered herself to her knees, running caressing hands over his sturdy thighs. Beside them, Shelley slid from her perch onto the floor, kneeling beside Kathryn, so they were eagerly eyeing the exposed waiting erections of their conquests.

They went to work in unison, stroking and sucking the stiff cocks and evoking moans and gasps from their men. Paul and Tom finally relaxed, making eye contact long enough to share a laugh; both were amazed to be in this situation, and now that the initial sensation of tension had passed, this felt bizarrely like the most natural thing in the world.

Kathryn was satisfied that Paul had managed to hold on to himself for longer than their meeting in the club toilet and worked him fervently, applying an expert technique to his considerable size.

Shelley couldn't resist. "Doing well, guys."

She stood up and turned her back to Tom, lowering her ass towards his groin, letting the head of his member brush against the white cloth of her panties, nuzzling between her cheeks, leaving a tendril of saliva and pre-cum on the material. Tom leaned forward unprompted and quickly slid those panties down past her knees, and before she could object he sank his face between her ebony buttocks.

"Oh, mine's hungry," she said, palms flat to the floor an inch in front of her feet, perfectly balanced as Tom slid his hands up her inner thighs and tickled her shaven sex. He bit the skin of her ass with gentle force then, as he slid a finger into her welcoming wet garden, he ran his tongue around the super-sensitive eye of her ass. She made a noise somewhere between a ticklish laugh and expressive pleasure. Through her yelps she managed: "Don't think for a second you're getting in there tonight, boy."

"*Now* you get prudish," he said, focusing on fingering her. She slid off him, dropping to her knees and he followed, hand finding its target again.

Kathryn turned her attention away from Paul, watching Shelley on all fours as Tom crouched behind her, thrusting fingers into her. Her brow was furrowed as if in concentration, enjoying the pleasure and not wanting to miss a single second of it. Her mouth was open, panting, her breath hot, her tongue just visible, and Kathryn was taken back to her bedroom last night, wanting again to feel that tongue lapping at her.

"Excuse me a tick," she told Paul and pivoted, sliding her thighs on either side of Shelley's body, hiking her hips up to present her tender area. Her dark-skinned friend gave her a knowing look, and eased herself forward, mouth wide open to cover Kathryn's pussy with hungry relish.

Paul watched Shelley's pink tongue writhing in the rent between Kathryn's legs, listening to the tiny splashing and slurping noises. Kathryn seemed to love the feeling, voicing her enjoyment: "Ah, yes, lick my clit. You know exactly how I like it."

Paul's hand went to his hard-on and he massaged it as he had done so hundreds of time before, holding back to avoid reaching the finish line, taking in every detail of the daisy chain of sexual activity in front of him; his best friend masturbating a girl on her knees, who in turn was going down on the girl who had brought him here tonight with the express purpose of having him. He was then suddenly struck with the reality of the situation; he was sitting back, watching it happen, and slowly jerking himself off.

"I'm a fucking spectator."

He swiftly dropped to the floor with them, penis thrust out, and he lowered his body towards Kathryn's face; she clasped the root of his potent piece and brought it to her mouth, sucking hungrily as he worked an exploring hand across her breasts. Shelley still dined at her moist buffet but snaked a hand out now, stroking Paul's thigh, a move that caught him by surprise. When that hand knocked Kathryn's away and squeezed his meat stick, he was powerless to do anything but go where she led, waddling with as much grace as possible while on his knees. Shelley brought his saliva-slick dick straight to her mouth and enveloped it, sliding it to the back of her throat so his balls rested on a chin still glossy with Kathryn's juice.

Kathryn rose up behind Paul and kissed his neck, hands going around to aid Shelley, tugging on his cock and guiding it into her mouth. From behind Shelley, Tom watched eagerly, and as if aware that he was missing an opportunity got to his feet and came around to where the action took place; without prompt, he slid his fingers through the tendrils of Kathryn's long hair, and pulled her mouth onto his rod.

With mutual juices shared and all barriers broken, everything was fair game. As Shelley sucked his dick like it contained an elixir, Paul pushed two fingers into Kathryn's hot snatch, and she held his wrist in place as she spat and choked on Tom.

"Tom," Shelley said sharply, her attention turning away from Paul, spit dribbling down her chin and spattering onto the carpet. He looked up, boner still being coated by Kathryn, thinking he was going to be told off, or asked to leave, but that wasn't to come. Shelley said: "Come and fuck me."

Kathryn stopped blowing him. "You'd better do what she says."

"Sit on the couch, now."

Tom did what he was told like a chastised schoolboy, tearing off his shirt as he went so he was completely naked, but for his socks. Shelley rocked on her hip. "And take those fucking things off."

He did, as Kathryn instructed Paul to sit next to him, and likewise strip off all the way. There they sat, completely naked, faced by women in lingerie, primed penises thrust skyward in anticipation of the ride of their lives.

Shelley turned her back to Tom as she had done earlier, two fingers coming down and parting her black pussy lips like a wrapper sliding off a sweet treat of pink candy. Tom's head ached in keenness, and he grabbed her hips to ease her down; she held his cannon solidly and rolled the moist cleft over its head, then ran the full length of her sticky slit down it, coating it in her sap.

"For fuck's sake, don't tease me," Tom begged.

"You love it."

Then she bade his head to break the surface of her sex and lowered herself onto him with urgency, all the way, both of them vocalising their passion.

"Fuck *me!*" Tom cried.

"That's the idea."

She rocked herself back and forth, hands on his knees, his white length reciprocating in her delicious quim. He kneaded the generous meat of her buttocks, gripped her black curls and pulled her hair so her back came flush with his chest, hands darting around to fondle her enormous breasts, freeing them fully from the corset, still standing out in stark contrast against her dusky skin.

Her legs came up and perched on the couch and she rose off him, then down, then off, then back again, riding him. When he noticed one of her hands go down to please her swollen clitoris, he knocked it away and gave her that pleasure himself.

In the short space of time it took them to get into position, Kathryn and Paul were just as busy. Kathryn straddled, facing him, offering up her pert little tits, which he caressed with his mouth, crying out a harsh breath as she lowered her slender weight onto his sturdy rock.

It felt incredible inside her, its girth filling her, and her hips rocked against him as it worked like a piston within those tight, scorching walls. She looked at him carefully; he was concentrating somewhat, holding back a climax.

"Don't come apart on me now, Paul," she whispered quietly in his ear, unheard over the moans of joy coming from her riding partner not two feet away. This struck enough of a chord with Paul that he clutched a handful of her hair and pulled her in very close, his mouth pressed to her ear, his words laced with quiet aggression.

"I think that's enough of the jokes. Now – it's simple really. Either you want me to fuck you, or you don't."

Hearing her own words spoken back to her filled her with a surge of pleasure, and the pressure of his hands in her hair turned her on. In reaction, she bucked her hips and rode faster, and he matched her movements with equal commitment.

"Fuck me," she said, simply and loudly.

Shelley's hand came over and grabbed Kathryn's neck and they moved to kiss each other, their pace never faltering as they bounced on their men.

Tom interrupted by pushing Shelley's feet off the couch and onto the floor, sliding out of her for long enough to place pressure on her shoulders, forcing her back onto her knees, bent over in front of him. He splayed her cheeks and spat a coursing rivulet into the dark chasm, watching his white liquid run down that valley and trickle through her dripping delta. Before it cast off to the floor, he grabbed her hips and hauled himself inside, pounding, balls swinging and slapping against his dick as it burst in and out of her tight cunt.

Kathryn followed suit and sprawled on all fours, stretching out on the couch as Paul entered her from behind, pounding with a rhythm she matched, coming back to meet every thrust.

The girls came a few beats apart; Shelley's her signature yelp, Kathryn's a silent, shuddering orgasm that filled her with white-hot energy. The boys paused as their women enjoyed the sensation; Kathryn looked back over her shoulder and smiled at Paul, a look that said 'That's what I've been waiting for.'

She slid herself off him and led him off the couch.

"You know what we should do now?" she said, stroking Shelley's hair and pivoting her back, so that Tom was forced to withdraw, slapping his cock against her sweat-coated ass cheeks.

"What's that?" Shelley asked breathlessly.

"Play a little game of take-your-pick. How about it, boys?"

For a game they had made up on the spot, everybody appeared to have an implicit understanding of the rules, certainly when Kathryn got onto her back and slid herself underneath Shelley, her head between the girl's thighs. Shelley quickly tilted forward and spread Kathryn's legs, mouths sinking into each other's glistening nooks in a perfect sixty-nine.

The men looked at each other, shrugged, and went to work.

Tom slid straight back into Shelley's ebony entrance and was rewarded with the sensation of Kathryn's tongue running along the underside of his length as he pumped, and the occasional full suck of each testicle in turn; Paul eased back Shelley's head and pushed his piece across her lips, lubing it up before plunging it back into Kathryn's waiting wet box.

They were four animals locked into one, each drawing endless pleasure from their actions, a sexual abandon they'd never experienced before. Everywhere they looked was bare flesh and fluids, a pornographic movie in three dimensions, played out in reality before their eyes. Every thrust and cry and stifled moan was vibrant and true.

Shelley spoke: "Kathryn, would you mind if I sampled your man?"

"Not at all," she said. "I wouldn't mind trying yours."

Paul and Tom shrugged, withdrew, and swapped ends as the girls continued feasting upon each other. Paul squatted behind Shelley's rump and Kathryn kissed his bulbous head and guided him in smoothly; Shelley's cavern was not as tight as Kathryn's, but no less delightful, and he drove in and out with equal joy. Tom let out a gritted-teeth rasp as he split open Kathryn's gates and made the journey into her moist tunnel, likewise noticing the difference but enjoying it no less.

They went through every permutation and combination; at times they were simply making smooth love to the girls' velvet passages, at others their mouths, and sometimes each girl was being filled out from both ends. The latter experience thrilled the girls no end, being in control and being used in equal measure.

Both of them came together, and Shelley's was violent enough to bring a small discharge of clear fluid from her, running across Paul's shaft and dripping into Kathryn's face. Kathryn was too busy having her own orgasm to notice.

When they broke their tightly-woven clinch, the girls lay flat on the floor, side by side, legs open, each one beckoning their original conquest to storm their waiting castles. Paul slid between Kathryn's tantalizing lips and she closed her calves around his ass, pulling him deeper; Shelley rested her thighs against Tom's chest as he entered, hooking the crook of her knees over his shoulders. He wrapped his forearms around her thighs as he pounded.

"So," Shelley said. "Who do you think was the best?"

Kathryn couldn't help but laugh. "I can't believe you're doing this now."

"Is this a competition?" Paul asked, sweat beaded across forehead and chest.

"Always, darling," Shelley said, then to Kathryn: "I bet I can make mine come before yours."

"That's not really a title a guy wants to win," Tom informed her.

Kathryn ignored him. "You're on." She looked straight into Paul's eyes. "Fuck me, Paul. Fuck me hard. I want you to come, I want you to shoot it all over me. I want to taste it."

Paul looked like a deer in the headlights, thrusting with a new urgency. Shelley was spurred on by Kathryn's vocal encouragement and added her own.

"Don't let these sad fools win, Tom, I want you now, I want you to spray my tits with your hot spunk. Come all over me and I'll lick up every drop." She rubbed her mammoth tits, squeezing them together, pointing her nipples towards him as if they were targets.

The men pounded and thrust as the girls called out their buzz.

"Fuck me!" Kathryn spat. "Are you going to come for me? I want that cum, I want to swallow it."

"Call yourself a man?" Shelley questioned. "Prove it, paste me with your cum, Tom."

Sweat coursed from their brows, falling on the girls' faces and chests. Shelley employed a dirty tactic and slid a hand down, pumping the root of Tom's member as he pounded; not to be outdone, Kathryn cradled Paul's balls, and slid a probing middle finger up between his cheeks, teasing his asshole.

Paul and Tom looked to be approaching the finish line in perfect unison, faces screwing up, pleasure manifest as grunts, and they threw themselves out of the girls and clambered to their final destinations.

Ropes of sticky jism burst forth from their aching dicks. Tom's draped across the black mountains at Shelley's chest, each spurt painting a new track across those epic globes. She traced her fingers through it and brought his salty gift to her mouth.

Paul's seed shot harpoon-like across Kathryn's lips and chin and she tasted him again for the second time in as many days, relishing the tang this time. He squeezed his gift onto her tongue and she accepted it gratefully.

Spent, the men rocked back on their haunches as the girls shared a final kiss, seed mixing; Shelley licked the last traces from Kathryn's lips, and Kathryn lapped up the rest of the pearly solution from Shelley's chest, feline and playful.

Finally they fell back to the carpet, heads pressed together as they surveyed their satisfied subjugates, the post-orgasmic feeling of self-consciousness now settling in. They looked a little embarrassed to be naked, sweating and drooping right next to each other.

"I think we'll have to call that a draw," Kathryn said, and the girls laughed together, knowing that competition would always continue between them, but that it was fine for them both to be the winner.

LANDSCAPE
A Poem

The landscape of your body
Is the focus of my trek.
Exploring, foraging, seeking
The exquisite beauty of your nature.

Valleys and peaks and rippling flesh,
Faint ridges of bone under fervent soil,
The tide of the ocean between
Rising, spreading cliffs.

I am time, eroding your fears.
I will crash against your shores,
Awash you with my will.
Let me be the storm, nourishing and fierce.

I roll through your wilderness,
And I wish to make my home
Amongst this pristine land, so
Ensnare me with your roots.

Pull me down, amongst your moisture,
Swallow and encompass every quivering
Inch of my devoted worship.
I grow strong amidst your love.

Envelop me, entwine,
Enfold me in your vines.
I'll make you my horizon,
So you're all I ever see.

EXTRA MARITAL PLEASURES

Louise sat in the back of the taxi, largely ignoring the inane ramblings of the driver, providing a few cursory conversational grunts and perfunctory 'oh really's?' to occupy him; her mind was elsewhere, happily trawling the events that had led to this cab ride. She had thought about very little else but the events of tonight, across the two days that she had not been in his presence, every second a blissful agony. She remembered everything all at once, how they had met and their first sexual encounter not two minutes later, but the prime memory was their most recent meet, the transitory, half-hour tête-à-tête that had left both of them clamouring for more of each other and setting up tonight with perfect precision. She still felt the same excitement now that she remembered feeling when Joseph, her newest and most wonderful friend, had named the day and date and added those magical words: "My wife won't be home until very late that night."

The cascade of butterflies she always felt when he spoke to her so suggestively span into a tornado within her. He had breathed the fact into her ear at close range in the way he had learned so quickly was a sure fire way to turn her on, speaking slowly, huskily, every word a promise of future fun.

She had reached out and clutched his tie then, pulling his handsome face closer, loving the rasping sensation of his immaculately trimmed goatee brushing her pale cheek. Squeezed into the booth in the cocktail bar that had become a frequent post-work hang out spot, she allowed him to nuzzle her neck and plant gentle kisses on her white flesh. The scattered patrons of the dark bar paid them no mind. Everyone in here was catching up with friends, drowning their post-work sorrows or, in the case of the more tactile couples, having fun behind somebody's back. They talked, teased and flirted, no doubt having chosen the place for the same reason Louise and Joseph had; it was dark, private and offered sanctuary to those entertaining extra marital dalliances and able to snatch a few scant moments with their new lovers in the ghost-space between finishing work and returning home to their real lives. Over in the corner of the bar, a resident pianist teased a languid jazz tune from the grand piano, providing a melodious soundtrack to the clandestine affairs taking place all around him.

"And what do you think we'll do?" Louise mused in response to his statement. The bristles of his beard were an opening salvo that heralded the arrival of his lips and he had peppered her throat with tiny pecks before returning to whisper in her ear.

"I want to ruin you in the bed I share with my wife."

She had quivered quite involuntarily at the prospect of the taboo concept. Joseph never talked of his wife or the more mundane aspects of the life he seemed so keen to seek solace from. Their relationship had been too short, fast and intense for an over abundance of conversation anyway, and what they did talk about where the things that were mutual loves for them both; rock music, popular culture and sex. Knowing that Joseph was married was a huge part of the allure for Louise; she was under no illusions that this whole tryst was based almost entirely on lust, on the danger and the passion inherent in the situation. The idea of lying with him in his marital bed made the flutter of excitement within her reach fever pitch.

His tailored grey pinstripe suit suited him so well, even though it was a world away from how he had looked during the first meeting: ripped jeans and a tight Rise Against T-shirt, dark with moisture across his toned chest where he had been part of the thronging crowd at the gig. This was Joseph in work mode, fresh from the office, and it was a good look on him.

His attention was rapt on her; he looked at her as if surveying a work of art, and she loved how that made her feel. She let his huge, brown eyes hold her in place as he took in her every inch, every buxom curve. She was proud of her full shape, knowing the power it had over the male populace; skinny models had nothing to hang on to and real men craved curvaceous ladies. Today's attire was her favourite work garb, a grey fitted skirt suit that perfectly showcased her hourglass figure. Her neat peplum jacket cinched her waist and flicked out over her stunning hips. The jacket was held in place with one button over a white blouse with a neckline she had widened with judicious unfastening, ever proud of her large, firm breasts that mesmerised any man lucky enough to gaze upon them. Her makeup was discreet but brought out the sparkle of her eyes, framed between square, black-framed glasses right out of a secretarial fantasy.

He ran a capable hand over her thighs, down past the hem of the short skirt, stroking the delicate material of her nylon holdups and tickling gently the sweet spot behind her knees that she so adored being attended to. She raised her legs to drape them over his, her black heels digging gently into the plush booth seating, toes bracing herself against the backrest as his hands sank across her toned calves. They soon began their return journey, slowly delving beneath her skirt and tracing across the dark band of her stockings before easing onto her flesh and burrowing closer to the flimsy white panties that she had worn especially for their short post-work meet.

"I want those beautiful, sweet lips on my cock," he said, his eyes never leaving hers, a commanding gaze. "I want you to bring me right to the edge then I'm going to spread you out on those sheets where I've lain with her for so long and lap away at you until you scream for mercy…"

She nodded, breath escaping in harsh rasps. Though she knew nobody in the bar could see them in this booth, she didn't care enough to make sure. She was in this moment with him, wishing this encounter could prolong itself into eternity rather than the ever-dwindling half hour they had before he had to return to his real life. No time to waste. She slid her cosseted ass across the seat towards his exploring fingers, feeling her own increasing wetness moistening the gusset of her panties and needing his contact. When it came she had to bite her lip to avoid screaming out. His tentative digits stroked the wet outline of her opening labia, teasing the delicate bud at the apex of her secret garden. She couldn't look away from his enrapturing stare, like a rabbit in blinding headlights. The pad of his thumb attended to her blossoming mound through her panties as his free fingers sought access beyond the gossamer threads.

The pianist's skilful fingers filled the air with a tinkling riff, but he was no match for Joseph's dexterous talent. He rolled the backs of his curled fingers through her shallow wet pool; here he held them, never delving within, denying her, teasing her, all the while making sure she knew how important she was in this dizzying encounter by watching her, *seeing* her, eyes never leaving her. He made her feel beautiful and in return she wanted to tear his trousers from him and descend onto the length she was becoming ever more addicted to…

She was still holding his tie and drew him in to kiss her as a sharp, distilled climax swept over her. She feasted hungrily on his lips and pushed her tongue into his smiling mouth, her hushed moans of pleasure lost beneath the ambient piano music. She braced her legs so hard that her heels ripped through the plush seating with a quiet renting of fabric. He kissed her until her orgasm had subsided, and continued beyond, cradling her legs and the small of her back, filling her with a contentment she had almost forgotten.

They said very little until it was time for them to part. They finished their drinks, left the bar and went out onto the busy evening street amidst the throng of commuters. With a swift, passionate embrace they went their separate ways, both facing two days without one another and facing the anticipation of a night alone. Still drifting in post-orgasmic bliss, that moment felt like it would never come.

But come it had, and as she paid the driver and stepped out of the cab, Louise was certain her heart was beating louder than the sound of her black heels clicking the concrete on the quiet suburban street. The vehicle slid off and she turned to face his home, a two storey house in a terrace of fine properties. The door was barely ten feet away, so much promise lying beyond it. She had worked out every step of the evening, plotted everything she was going to do to him like a sprawling erotic novel. First she would treat him, get on her knees and transport him to a world of delights he'd never even contemplated.

She strode up to the door and rang the bell.

*

Louise loved the expression on Joseph's face when they would meet. He always smiled, but with his whole body, a gesture she had forgotten was possible. The smile made his effortlessly approachable face even more open and inviting. It went to the very core of him, changing his posture. He *swelled* to be around her. It made his dark eyes seem so glow from within, and made her feel all the more wonderful that it was all for her.

Joe wore a plain light blue shirt tucked into dark chinos, casual but ineffably smart, and he ushered her across the threshold, marveling at her in his quiet, attentive way. She wore one of her most expensive coats for him, her knee-length black Georgia Mae frock coat, buttoned up to her pale neck, dove skin standing out in sharp contrast and inviting him to kiss it, which he refrained from doing until she had completely revealed herself.

"You look stunning," he said earnestly.

"Wait until you've seen it all before you go making snap judgments," she teased, unfurling the slimline belt-tie from around her waist, drawing attention to her eminently desirable hips. She threw the coat open and he helped her slide her arms out of it, hanging it on the hook.

"No, I was definitely right," Joe assured her. She twirled for him to show off her outfit, her torso clad in a cinching purple corset that alternated between lilac, lavender and navy blue as she span for him. An intricate series of bows laced up across her spine, and a large black blow rested snugly on the cusp of the garment between her large breasts, emphasised by the corset so as to be astonishingly full, quivering slightly with each movement and drawing Joseph's eye. Her spin revealed her exposed shoulder blades and the wonderful tattoo across the right one, a detailed rendition of a famous feminine cat burglar clad in her latex catsuit, seemingly scratching through Louise's own flesh with her gleaming claws, leaving three detailed, jagged scars traced in red and black ink. Louise's love for geek culture was an innate part of her appeal to Joe.

Completing the outfit was a denim miniskirt clinging to her voluptuous hips and cut off at the thigh to expose a narrow strip of white flesh above the ornate, dark band of her customary sheer holdups. She had chosen these because of the narrow black seam that ran up the backs of her legs; Joseph had explained his love for ladies in hosiery during a post-work conversation and she loved to dress up for him. The black heels made every muscle in her legs look taut and ready to be used.

The look on Joseph's face suggested he couldn't believe his luck and it excited Louise afresh. She had dressed for him in a way she knew his wife never would, and all the better because it was her natural state: an urban rock chick that looked ready for all kinds of noisy, extreme fun. Her display completed, he pulled her close with an all-encompassing hug and kissed her deeply, soaking her ruby red lip stain into his own lips. She was slightly shorter than him and went onto tip-toes, one leg rising behind her involuntarily the way she had seen in the movies, and never thought possible until kissing the right man, a man like Joe who existed here only for her, to worship and ruin her in all the right ways.

"Come through," he said, leading her by the hand into the living room. Her imaginings of the house matched almost perfectly with what she saw. The living room had hardwood floors and through a wide archway was the dining room; what had once been two rooms had been knocked into one. The kitchen was white with black appliances. Joseph had a job in finance and his wife was a solicitor; without kids, they lived within their means but clearly lived well.

There were photos of them together adorning the walls, Joseph looking handsome and contented, his wife smiling in some, looking glacial in others. She reminded Louise of somebody that she couldn't place, perhaps a celebrity. She was certainly beautiful but with an austerity, hair always immaculate, her clothing always perfectly pressed and presentable to the point of...was artifice the word she was thinking of? She had short blonde hair bobbed to her chin, a contrast to Louise's dark tresses spilling down her back, a back which Joseph now caressed with deft fingers, drawing her attention away completely from his married life.

"Would you like some wine?" he asked.

Louise didn't hesitate. "No. I want to take you to bed."

They rushed like giddy teenagers up the stairs, past more photos of the so-called happy couple, bursting into the bedroom. Louise took it in quickly. It was spacious, with a king sized bed and two walk-in wardrobes that she fully imagined Joseph's wife was in full control of. A small en-suite bathroom was nestled away to the side and the lady of the house's vanity table dominatded the wall opposite the foot of the bed. The art pieces on the wall were non-specific abstract swatches, the kind available in bulk in home furnishing stores. A bedside table on each side of the bed held a selection of books from wildly apposite authors.

"There doesn't seem to be a whole lot of you in this room," Louise mentioned.

"There isn't a whole lot of me in this *house*, sometimes," he said, throwing himself into the plush white quilt and watching her look around. She felt a strange sense of melancholy approaching. Not guilt, because she had long since managed to reconcile that; they were both adults, and Joseph was keen to pursue, so any guilty feelings should rest with him. It was something akin to sadness at seeing a marriage being lived out under the illusion of perfection when both parties were so clearly unhappy.

You don't know anything about his wife, she thought. *Maybe she's perfectly satisfied by all of this...* She thought about asking what his wife would think if she knew about their dalliance, but the moment would evaporate faster than she could finish the sentence. Instead she rocked on her hip and placed a finger to her lower lip.

"So what are we going to do, Mr. Smith?"

"Come over here, I'm sure we'll think of something."

She crawled onto the bed and positioned herself over him, the curls of her hair drifting across his body then tickling his face; she imagined them intertwining with the tiny bristles of his beard, becoming one, drawing her close and she acted accordingly, lowering to kiss him. In her straddled position, bent low, he had full access to every ample inch of her. His able hands slid across her corset to her hips, round to her buttocks, squeezing through the denim skirt then sinking lower to her nylons where he instinctively traced the seams.

"You're so sexy," he told her. "I just want to scream it out loud."

"Oh, you're going to be screaming, all right." Louise winked at him, nimble fingers unfastening the buttons of his jeans and he shuffled to allow her to slide them off, tugging off shoes and socks as she went and discarding everything in an unkempt heap on the bedroom floor, leaving him only in a shirt and checkered boxers, already bulging out of shape with the aroused meat within. She kissed the bulge, nuzzled it with her nose in an animalistic gesture, even growled playfully and bared her teeth around the hidden tube of flesh.

She slid off his shorts and let his eight inch cock free, ready for her touch. She blew a narrow cone of air across it, watching it respond, his freshly shorn scrotum tightening under the chilly breath.

"Cold in here, isn't it?" she joked, then kissed him gently, putting lingering pecks from root to tip across the lower side of his rod, leaving beautiful lipstick marks across the peach skin. Her hands stretched up to his shirt, unbuttoning it slowly, deliberately; as long as there was still buttons fastened she would not take him fully into her mouth, and she made sure he understood this, working at a snail's pace, slapping his hand away when he tried to help. She looked at him through her black-framed glasses and she felt his dick twitch against her chin; that made her smile, knowing then she could arouse him with a simple *glance*. She stroked a hand up his smooth abdomen and through the light smattering of hairs on his chest, rasping through his beard and into his open mouth. He sucked her finger and she ran it, wet with his saliva, all the way back down his body and across his length.

He shrugged himself free of the shirt, completely naked while she remained fully clothed. From their conversation she knew he loved this, being exposed with a woman allowed to take total control of him. It was time to play.

In a fluid motion she took his majestic cock into her mouth and sucked it all the way to the root, rousing an unrestrained moan of pleasure from him: "Oh, fucking hell, Louise!" He propped himself up on his elbows to watch her skilful ministrations, gliding her perfect mouth up and down him, encompassing him completely. One hand sank to his balls, cupping with control, massaging them. Her other hand gripped his shaft and worked it as she devoted her mouth to his throbbing helmet, sucking in quick motions as if to draw succor from it. He writhed under her expert technique, gasping and calling her name, telling her how beautiful and wonderful she was.

"Hold my hair," she told him. "Never let me go until I make you come."

"But, what about you?"

"Plenty of time for that," she said between hungry mouthfuls of his pulsing member.

He obliged, taking her curls between his fingers and gripping tightly as if holding on for dear life. He applied pressure to work her head rhythmically, although she needed no guidance.

She adored this feeling, of using her mouth to provide such delight. She had always been obsessed with pleasuring others this way, an oral fixation that had carried with her since giving her first blowjob in her late teens, to an eager young man who had almost screamed the house down. Seeing that reaction had elated her as it did now; she could feel blood coursing to her loins, loving how she could turn herself on with the simple application of suction and saliva. The taste sensations that came with it were incredible and addictive to her, the saline tang of his oozing pre-cum and the full load soon to follow.

"You're amazing," he told her. "Amazing in every way."

She took his meat from her mouth and grinned, admiring her handiwork, the prominent veins across his member, the sheen of wetness she had given him. His bell-end looked full, strained and polished like a delicious plum. She kissed it, smearing her lipstick across him. She flicked her tongue over the taut fleshy string between his glans and shaft, eyes sparkling.

"Do you like this corset?" she purred.

"It might just be the best thing I've ever seen," he laughed.

She guided his dick along the top, tracing saliva along the black lining and through the curls of the bow, then gently tapped him against the squeezed flesh of her breasts, rippling with each strike. They were large normally but this corset made them seem like planets unto themselves nestled there, bound in silk, teetering on the edge of spilling out but held, teasingly steady. She pointed his rod against its natural grain towards his feet and he shifted to allow her to thread his meat into the squeezed canyon of her cleavage, the corset providing all the hold that was needed for wonderful resistance. She rocked on her knees, staying low, giggling in delight at this new found variation on masturbating a man with her breasts. To come at him from the other angle would be better, and would allow him access to her moistening folds, but there was no need to rush anything. She rather enjoyed seeing him strain in discomfort and pleasure.

She slid him free and his dick sprang back against his stomach with a strident, wet slap. She descended on him again and felt him reach that point of total arousal, everything tightening. She had seen that familiar look in his eyes a few times these past few weeks, in hotel rooms and toilet cubicles, and knew he was close. The stark naked man writhed beneath her. She would deny him no longer.

"You don't have to hold back. We have all night. Give it to me. Give me your spunk."

The dirty words were the final straw and she sank her mouth over his cock just in time, applying a few final, deepthroating bobs to make him lose all control. Like a dam bursting he came with a glorious cry of orgasmic joy, unable to contain himself. His seed gushed onto the moist cushion of her tongue and she undulated her throat to take it deep inside her, swallowing every drop pumping from his pulsing pipe.

She gasped, spilling a tendril of glistening gossamer down her chin, catching it with a nimble finger and scooping it back inside, tongue lapping it up as Joseph could only watch in awe, panting to suck oxygen into his overworked lungs. His forehead and torso were beaded with sweat and he looked sated, but she knew him well enough sexually by now to know what those eyes meant.

It was her turn, and he would never skimp on the attention he lavished upon her.

"Come here, you fabulous minx," he ordered, kissing her deeply, uncaring that he could still taste himself on her wicked tongue. He buried his face into the dramatic tray of her cleavage, moving his face back and forth with a growl and causing her to laugh merrily at his goofiness, but his true destination never wavered. He rolled her onto her back and slid her denim skirt up, bunching it round her waist to reveal, to his open mouthed, grinning delight, that she was wearing no panties.

"Is something wrong?" she said with faux consternation.

"Oh, nothing at all," he said, parting her thighs and holding her legs flat to the bed, hands restraining her. He kissed the white hollow of flesh on either side of her exposed, tantalising snatch, her lips already open for him, glistening and appetising, her clitoris engorged by her own oral act and ready for his own.

His tongue was inches away, ready to lap, when they heard the front door of the house open and slam closed.

The sound was eerily noisy in the sudden silence caused by two people holding their breath. Two sets of eyes went wide and two bodies froze in perfect unison as a woman's voice called out in the stillness.

"Hi Joe," she said and they heard footsteps in the hallway and the sounds of her shrugging off her coat. Without waiting for a response she continued. "Maria and Sally can't make it because they've come down with some stomach bug or something or other, and Mike's kid has broken his arm so we're postponing the meal until everybody's better. I'll order takeout so I hope you're – " Joe's wife's words stopped and they could almost hear her thinking.

Within a second they could hear her footsteps coming hurriedly up the stairs and this was finally the thing that galvanised them into action. As Joe darted to the bathroom and swung a towel around his waist, Louise sprang from the bed like a coiled spring and took three silent, gazelle-like steps into one of the walk-in wardrobes, pulling the door shut behind her and taking cover behind a colourful array of hanging dresses. She held her breath, suddenly realising just how absurd the situation was, and cursed herself for ever thinking it was a good idea to meet here.

Stay on neutral ground, she thought. *Why the fuck did you come here, you stupid girl? Stay quiet, stay hidden, you might just get through this without having your hair ripped out or breaking a girl's heart…*

Joe's wife had reached the top of the stairs at full pelt and strode into the bedroom. Louise listened to Joe emerging from the bathroom.

"Hi, I was just about to hop in the shower," he said innocently. "Shame about your night out. You could come in the shower with me if you like?"

Light at the end of the tunnel… Louise thought in the gloom, and then came the words that suggested that light was a train coming her way:

"Whose coat is that hanging up downstairs?" Her voice was steely and cold.

Joseph stammered. "Wh – what coat? Is there a coat?"

"A frock coat that certainly isn't mine. Nobody I know wears a coat like that."

"Didn't your sister leave it last time she was – "

"It's not my sister's," she said icily, then left a deadly beat. "Who is she and where is she?"

"Sophie, I don't know what you're – "

"Who is she and where is she, Joseph?" she demanded, each word a venomous barb. Joseph had no answer, and that's when Louise heard Sophie's feet moving to the bathroom, searching.

"Sophie, this is crazy," she heard Joseph protest, but Sophie was already at the first walk-in wardrobe adjacent to the one Louise was taking cover in, shoving the door open. "You're being illogical."

"Am I?" Sophie said. "Then why are you sweating, Joe? Big

exertion, turning on the shower is it?"

"I've been exercising," he defended smoothly as Sophie slid clothes along the racks

"I bet." She heard Sophie patting the quilt they had left somewhat unkempt from their encounter. "Do sit ups on the bed, do you?"

Louise's brain worked twice as fast as usual, knowing that Sophie was about to find her. She refused to be found cowering, and though she wouldn't go on the offensive, because she was far from a position in which she could adopt the moral high ground, she would at least tackle the problem head on.

Come on Lou, let's face the music.

She swept the clothes aside and came face to face with Sophie on either side of the threshold to the wardrobe, bringing Joseph's wife to a standstill. She was taller than Louise, slimmer through the hips, bordering on too skinny. She was wearing an above-the-knee crepe dress of a rich magenta, cinched at the waist by a thin black belt. Three quarter length sleeves gave way to slender wrists and hands balled into fists. She looked rather beautiful for her now-cancelled evening, her face set with a mix of anger, surprise and restraint; it was also a face that Louise recognised, and the vague familiarity from the photos throughout the house now crystallised at the same time as did Sophie's own recognition. Their faces had changed only slightly in the twenty years since they had last seen each other, when both had been wearing school uniforms.

"Hi, Sophie," Louise said as neutrally as she could manage.

Sophie's demeanour sagged a little. "Louise?"

Across the bed, Joseph looked completely confused. "You two know each other?"

"We went to school together," Sophie said, her eyes never leaving Louise's face, her fists still clenched, ready to swing. "How long has this been going on? And please, don't insult my intelligence and try to pretend that you aren't fucking each other."

The women had never looked away from one another. Louise refused to cower or run, and would offer any answer the woman wanted to hear; this was not the time to try and be smart, or sarcastic, or mean. Though they had never been real friends at school, they had never been enemies, and Louise was certain they had shared a moment of understanding or two during their school tenure, so would offer her the courtesy of explaining an unexpected situation she no doubt found crushing.

"Almost three weeks," Louise explained. "Three weeks this coming Wednesday."

Sophie calculated it lightning fast: "The Alice Cooper gig."

"Yes."

She was still icily calm, anger contained, bubbling but in check. "What happened?"

"We danced, we talked, we swapped numbers," Joseph said, trying to insert himself in the conversation of which he was the subject, though feeling like he was barely part of the proceedings at all.

"And we had sex in the toilet stall," Louise added, refusing to hide anything. "We've met four times since then before tonight and one of those was a night in a hotel room. The other times were quick meets after work." Sophie was building the picture in her mind. "Sophie, I know this comes as a shock and an apology will sound disingenuous, but I'm sorry you found out this way. We knew exactly what we were doing."

Sophie's jaw was set and static, her eyes remarkably free of even the faint prickle of tears. Whether or not she was so collected that she rarely showed emotion, or if she was just in shock at the situation, Louise couldn't tell. Finally she looked across at her husband, standing awkwardly in his towel.

Her words came out in such a matter-of-fact manner, she might as well have been commenting on the weather. "I've been sleeping with Mike for two months."

Now it was Louise's turn to shift her gaze to Joseph, whose reaction surprised her just as much as Sophie's to the recent revelations.

He shrugged his bare shoulders. "I know."

Sophie nodded slightly. "You know. Of course you know. I was never good at hiding anything. The girls don't have a stomach bug. I thought that was clever. It was just supposed to be me and Mike. But his kid really *does* have a broken arm." Her fists finally unclenched and she flapped her palms against her slender hips. "My running about behind your back goes south on me, and I end up finding out about yours. Irony will get you every time."

The dynamic between Joseph and Sophie was one Louise couldn't entirely fathom; clearly unhappy and with deceit on both sides, but a sense of resigned certainty to getting on with things, even if those things were a loveless marriage and a string of infidelities. She almost felt a pang of regret wondering if there had been mistresses for Joseph before herself, but that kind of thinking was unfair; he certainly wasn't the first married man she had been with. Stable, monogamous relationships had never worked for her. One day her attitude might change, but she was young and having fun, and would change for nobody.

Sophie sank into the bed, hands in her lap. The toes of her black high heels clicked together absently, as if willing herself with three magic clicks to be swept away to a different world. Joseph gradually came around the bed and sank down next to his wife, still clad in only a towel.

"It's broken," he said. "I know."

"And what does it say that I'm not even angry about it?"

Louise watched them share a look that held the tenderness of familiarity, but an uncertainty of what the future now held for them. This was not her business any longer and, swallowing her disappointment that her fleeting relationship with Joseph had come to an abrupt end, she made a move to exit.

"I'll leave you two alone."

Sophie patted the vacant quilt to her right and looked up at her with hopeful eyes. "Sit down."

"I should leave you two to – "

"Just sit with us a while," Sophie said. "I'm not going to freak out, I promise." She patted the duvet again and a smile crossed her lips. "Really, sit down. You still see anybody from school?"

Louise sat down, third in a huddled row in the silent bedroom.

"Not really, I drifted apart from everyone."

"So did I," Sophie explained. "I miss how totally fucking simple it was back then. It seemed so complicated when you're there but you realise how easy you had it when you grow up."

"Tell me about it," Louise said.

After some wistful, silent reminiscing Sophie said: "Do you remember Danny Franklin's parties?"

This brought a genuine smile to Louise's face. "I do. Well, some of them. I used to get rather merry."

"Did you two hang out?" Joseph ventured.

"We were never really friends," Sophie said. "But we got on in passing. Never close enough to bitch about or bully each other. I remember one of those parties where we ended up in a circle together playing spin the bottle."

Louise racked through a haze of twenty year old memories, searching for the same recollection and successfully finding it, picturing Sophie with shaggy hair sitting across from her in a circle of drunken teenagers amidst a throng of others dancing and drinking. "Oh yeah!" she said. Following the memory through she saw Sophie spin the bottle, watched it twirl on the carpet and come to rest pointing straight at her.

"The boys always went wild when a girl landed on a girl, and they always expected you to go for it."

"And you really did," Louise said, recalling how Sophie had crawled in the way that drunken teens think is sensual across the intervening space and kissed Louise on the mouth, a kiss she had reciprocated, gently at first and then, spurred on by the cheers of the boys in the room, had lashed their tongues deeply into each other's mouths for several seconds before breaking off, giggling and wiping their lips.

"I was pretty drunk," Sophie conceded. "Don't think we really spoke much after that, but I thought about it sometimes when I saw you."

Louise looked at her then, and saw a woman who had never explored any number of fleeting or lingering feelings, keeping them bottled up inside until it had spilled over into a confused marriage and sexual secrets. Sophie looked back with a surprising twinkle in her eye.

"What are you thinking?" Louise said, and a tentative hand drifted to Sophie's knee, patting her opaque tights with reassuring pressure.

"I'm thinking 'fuck it'," Sophie told her. She looked at her husband. "We were both going to do something really naughty and wrong tonight. Why stop now?"

Sophie's own hand drifted to the opaque black tights encasing her Louise's thigh, sliding up under the hem of her denim skirt.

She tilted her head and closed her eyes, mouth slightly parted waiting for Louise to kiss her, to finish what they had started twenty years ago.

Louise hesitated in silent disbelief at how events had shifted, and was thankful that there had been no tears, tantrums, or clumps of hair ripped out by vengeful brides. If the truth had come to light between the couple about their infidelities, then acceptance was something they'd have to deal with. If Sophie's repressed sexual urges and desires was a direct consequence, and she was as eager as she appeared, then Louise was not going to refuse. Sophie had cost her an orgasm once tonight, and appeared willing to provide her with a replacement.

Louise reciprocated, her lips lightly brushing against Sophie's to test if it was what she truly wanted; when Sophie persisted and returned the kiss, her desire was evident. She stroked further up Louise's thigh, as their adroit tongues carried on a wonderful courtship, and Louise ran a hand up Sophie's back, fingers tip-toeing across the pearls of her spine before holding her neck and kissing her more deeply.

Joseph, mind slowly acclimating to the goings on before him, reached out a hand to his wife's thighs, teasing her dress upwards. Sophie broke the kiss and spoke in her habitual, cool tone: "Just watch. I want her to myself for now, like you've had her."

Duly chastised he backed off, moving from the bed to the chair at the vanity table, turning it to face the erotic proceedings between his mistress and his wife. Sophie stood and turned her back to Louise, arms primly at her sides. "Unzip me."

Louise obeyed, sliding the zipper down with a satisfying sound, exposing Sophie's back in a widening V shape, intersected by the black band of her bra. The blonde woman shrugged it from her shoulders and slithered to allow the dress to fall swiftly, her thin hips offering little resistance until a pink pool of fabric formed at her feet. She was wearing opaque black tights that juxtaposed beautifully with her white skin, and she bent, ballerina-like, untying the straps of her heels and stepping fluidly from them.

Louise tried her luck, wrapping her arms around the slender woman's waist and pulling her down onto the plush duvet, making Sophie yelp a little in surprise, but she wore a satisfied smile as she stretched languidly beneath Louise, who assumed the same position she had with Joseph not ten minutes earlier. Where Joseph had wrapped his arms around Louise and caressed her body while they kissed, Sophie did the opposite, spreading her arms above her and offering little opposition as their lips united. Louise held her wrists in place, nuzzling her neck as Sophie's eyes drifted close, breathing quietly, mouth twitching into a smile. Her perfume was subtle enough to plant its scent in ones nostrils and create the need for constant resampling.

I wonder how ticklish she is...

Louise ran nimble fingers down the outside of Sophie's arms, all the way to her abdomen, feeling the tiny lady buck gently against her and give a breathy giggle, but her arms did not snap down the way they would if she was against this. This urged Louise to plant her kisses across her new lover's shoulders and arms then head south. She pressed lips gently to the hollow of her underarm, shaven clean for the man who would not get to taste her this evening; Louise loved that she was reaping the benefits of Sophie's rigourous preparation and preening. A woman's regime preparing for a night that would lead from seduction to sex was sacred, delicate and thorough, and Sophie was no exception.

Downward she moved, kissing the exposed mounds of flesh resting snugly within the cups of her lacy black bra, then moving on to each imperceptibly pronounced rib until she reached the taut waistband of her stockings. Still she kissed, loving the sensation of nylon against her lips; she clutched the crook of Sophie's knees and attentively pecked her thighs through the thick denier membrane before similarly coating her calves.

Louise let her tongue roll out and trace across the tops of Sophie's feet while her fingers were tickling her heels gently. She looked at Sophie over her glasses; the wife's eyes were closed, relishing the sensation. She glanced over at Joseph, still perched in his seat, wrapped in his fake-disguise bath towel, watching with total interest. They finally shared a look of surprise.

When she had kissed each of Sophie's toes in turn she applied pressure to roll her on to her stomach and began the return journey. Over her calves to the crook of her legs she went, the material offering too much protection to that most sensitive of areas.

"Forgive me, I'll buy you a new pair," Louise said, pinching the material and ripping it, exposing the back of her knees, a shallow trough that begged for her care. She crisscrossed her tongue slowly through that pale glade, drawing a pleasing, melodic laugh from Sophie. She moved higher, repeating her tearing gesture to rent the material, licking the flesh exposed through the tights until she got to Sophie's taut buttocks, which she nibbled gently, tugging at the nylon with her teeth, stretching it until it tore.

Sophie's legs parted, revealing the faint outline of her sex, the material darkening where it made contact with that opening door. Louise worked a finger through the nearest rent and wormed it closer, down across the tight seal of her ass and to the moist lips, easy and divine to penetrate. Immediately Sophie exhaled sharply, gripped the edge of the bed and raised her stomach from the quilt, the orbs of her buttocks sealed in slashed nylon, presenting themselves to Louise, inches away from her face.

She spoke to her husband now, who was transfixed by what was happening but forbidden from interfering, his own sexual partner being used as a lure. "Do you like watching?"

Joseph nodded.

"Prove it," his wife said, and Louise watched too as he discarded his towel, revealing the rod still bearing the final traces of her drying saliva, already impressively engorged once more. "Did she suck it? Does she suck it like I rarely ever do? I bet those lips feel great…"

It was an invitation for Louise to apply those skilful lips to her raised and waiting sliver, still encased within damp nylon. Any feelings of awkwardness were outstripped by Louise's love of being part of this game between lovers. Her heart was racing, blood coursing back to her own pussy to bring that beautiful sheen to those lips.

She wrenched the nylon over Sophie's quim with two hands, exposing it like a meal for a starving soul, and Sophie rocked back to greet Louise's open mouth and agile tongue. It had been several months since Louise had been with a woman and the delight at tasting that musky sweetness always anointed her afresh; being with women was a treat, a delicacy, a wonderful vacation from the men she entertained. Sophie's back arched as Louise dined on her pussy; she breathed rhythmically, restraining any sounds of pleasure

"I can see why you like her so much, her mouth is amazing." Sophie said. Joe's hand went to his erection and gripped it at the base, stroking the lower few inches, forcing his bulbous head to swell even harder. "How come you never get that hard for me?"

"You never seem like you want it," Joseph said.

"I always fucking want it…" she said and there was a seething anger present there. Not wanting this to turn into a series of recriminations, Louise spread Sophie's nylon-wrapped buttocks to allow her deeper, Sophie nestling her wet snatch against the stranger's lips and chin, grinding coolly against the slippery intruder. Her ambrosia seeped into Louise's mouth as her breaths became more erratic, plunging closer to an orgasm. Louise knew it was coming and felt her own burning desire increase; regardless of gender it was a marvel to bring off someone with her mouth. *Her* mouth. Her skills, her precision and touch.

Sophie released one single cry, stifled by biting gently into the back of her hand, the muscles in her thighs tensing then quivering as her climax came and receded. She slid into a flat position on the bed, legs bending at the knee and dancing back and forth a second in a post-orgasmic display of glee. She rolled over with grace, hands drifting through her hair, tousling it with satisfied strokes.

I hope she kisses me to taste herself... Louise thought, willing Sophie to take her face in her hands and plant those lips against hers, but Sophie had other plans. With a force Louise would never have guessed she possessed, she took the brunette by the back of her neck and bent her husband's mistress over her knees.

"Let's get you out of these restrictive clothes," Sophie said. "Do you want me to undress your new little plaything?"

Her husband massaged his pole and gave her a nod.

Louise allowed her hips to rise a little so that Sophie could unzip her skirt and slide it down, revealing her pleasingly plump ass cheeks and the full glory of her holdups, an intricate band of spiderweb running the perimeter of her thighs. When she was free of the skirt and lying flat across the smaller girl's legs, giving voluntarily the total control of the situation, a shiver ran through her as Sophie turned her attention to her corset.

She unfastened it one ribbon at a time, and Louise felt extra air rushing into her lungs as each bond was relaxed. Sophie wore an expression like a child on Christmas morning unwrapping a gift that they already knew the identity of, trying to hold in their excitement.

"She's gorgeous, isn't she? Sophie asked her husband as he slowly worked his thick cock.

"You are too," he said, and Louise could see in his eyes that he meant it. She fathomed that this was the kind of attitude he rarely saw from his wife, the kind of sexual liberation he craved, as all men did, and when it had not been forthcoming he had sought it elsewhere. Being presented with his wife as a prowling, take-charge vixen was like a galvanizing flame. Their exchange suggested as much.

"We stopped treating each other like objects a long time ago," Sophie mused, attentively releasing the last of the corset's bonds. "We got too comfortable and stopped having this much fun…"

"I'm sorry for looking elsewhere," Joe blurted out, and it seemed to surprise him.

"No, you're not," Sophie said with zero melancholy. "Just as I'm not, either. We always were perfect for each other."

With the last ribbon loosened, Louise allowed herself to be released from the corset, a vibrant butterfly released from its fetishised cocoon. Her huge breasts were free and she arched her back to permit Joseph a look of those tits that he had ably caressed during their tryst. She felt Sophie trace the outline of her comic-book tattoo, scratching her nails against the inked slashes the anti-hero had made.

"I had fantasies about you after that kiss," Sophie told Louise, thin fingers now coiling her hair. "It was my only experience with a girl and I've always fantasized about going further. I guess you made an impression, because usually the fantasies were about you…"

"You only had to give me a call," Louise said. "I'd have been there to play in a heartbeat."

"I'm glad it was you my husband decided to play with," she said. "But that doesn't change the fact of how naughty it was."

Louise felt Sophie leaning over towards her bedside table, and looked back over her shoulder to see her old school peer spill the stack of books to the floor and securely grip the largest one, a sturdy hardback which she clutched along its shortest edge and brandished like a paddle.

"And naughty girls need to be shown the error of their ways, don't they?"

"They do," Louise said willingly, relishing the anticipation of that book being used in a way that would make its author blush.

"They do, indeed," Sophie agreed.

Louise was certain she heard the blade of Sophie's arm *swish* through the air as she brought the broadside of the book down hard across her right buttock with a slap that echoed throughout the silent house. She couldn't hold in her excited yelp and loved the sensation of her ass cheek rippling, spreading the wave across her thigh from the epicentre of exquisite, stinging pain where the book had made contact.

The book came down three times again on the same cheek in quick succession, harder each time, then four times on the untouched cheek, bringing fresh, delightful smarting with every blow. Louise cried out and seethed through gritted teeth as the blows increased in strength.

"Naughty girl, you lead so many people astray," Sophie said breathlessly, soothing the reddening skin with her flat palms, kneading fingers into Louise's ass. She looked at her husband. "Come here."

He stalked to the bed with intent to cause sexual mischief of the highest order. He had left the towel behind and was now fully presented, exposed and erect, shaft bobbing with every step until he halted in front of his wife, Louise's body a barrier between them.

"Tell her why you chose her. Why her, over the hundreds of other girls you pass every day? Don't tell her it was because of me. Tell her why it was because of *her*."

Joe hesitated only a second until he realised how serious his wife was, then he dropped to his knees to bring his face level with Louise's.

"It's because she was so alive when I first saw her," Joseph said, speaking directly to Louise and it thrilled her how he talked about her as if she wasn't here, all the while never taking his eyes off her. "She was so sexy and she didn't seem to care who was looking at her. The attention was secondary. She was just being *her*, dancing on her own for her own benefit. She was so sexy."

His words were so beautiful that Louise felt a surge of emotion welling up alongside her intense arousal; she hadn't realised until now just what she had meant to Joseph, about what their relationship represented. She hadn't realised how he had watched her long before they had met amidst the throng of the crowd.

Sophie was enraptured by the story, and her spanking ceased.

"Tell me how it happened. Tell me everything."

PERFECT PLEASURES

*

Louise loved this feeling, being a part of crowd, all surging together as one. In the vast arena there were fifteen thousand people all with the same goal, sharing the same air, dancing, writhing sweating and singing as before them, up on the stage before a halo of multicoloured lights was the target of their affections, a true god of rock. He stalked the stage in leather pants and a long flowing black coat, tearing the roof off the place with a voice that had only gotten better in all the years that he'd been doing it. She loved how Alice Cooper was still doing it infinitely better than acts half his age.

She had fought her way almost to the front, part of the mass of leaping, grinding bodies. Coming alone was never a problem for her; few of her friends shared her musical taste and she rather liked being unique, and being able to cut loose at these concerts without anybody judging her. Everybody else in the cavernous venue was there for the same reason and it felt good. She was wearing PVC boots up to her knees, fishnet tights beneath a short leather mini skirt, and a tight tour T-shirt from another of her favourite acts. It hugged her huge breasts and made all of the rock boys stare as she threw her arms high or clutched her hips to grind against the crowd.

She became aware of a tall man to her right, her shoulder rubbing his sturdy upper arm. She turned towards him and felt a rush of delight at how attractive he was; tall, well-toned and wrapped in a Rise Against T-shirt and a pair of torn jeans. The shirt was damp with the accumulated sweat of a thousand strangers, and that was arousing to her as his fine taste in tunes. He had an immaculately trimmed goatee, his short hair was styled to perfection, and he glowed with exertion. She wouldn't learn that his name was Joseph until later, but the attraction was instant, and he was somewhat mesmerised by her. She was used to being eyed up in places like this, but that he had eyes only for her when there were a dozen leggy blonde rock chicks in daisy dukes within ten feet was a compliment and a turn on. She thought of speaking to him but being this close to so many amplifiers at a rock gig made it impossible to hear anything other than the music and the roar of the crowd.

Give him a show, she thought. She always lost her inhibitions at gigs like this, without the need for a single drop of alcohol. This was a natural rush, better and truer than any other. At the end of every gig she always rushed home to pleasure herself, to feel the atmosphere and pressure of the crowd, the smell of so many bodies roiling together, the music still ringing in her ears. It made her wet just to think of it.

She turned her back to him and stepped closer, grinding her hips against his thighs, inviting him to lay his hands all over her in rhythm with Alice's latest sleaze-rock masterpiece. His hands went to her hips and pulled her close, and through her leather skirt she could feel his impressive bulge. Every time she thrust back to meet him she felt it increase in size and rigidity, rising thanks to her. She turned to face the tall gentleman, unable to resist lifting a leg and hooking it over a hip and pressing against him, hiking her skirt up to allow the rapidly moistening gusset of her panties to feel that swell. They were so close to the people around them that nobody noticed, incapable of looking down as the band held their total attention, working their lyrical magic.

He was a little stunned at how forward she was being, but he didn't resist, cupping her buttocks through the shiny leather and drawing her closer, rubbing the tent of his jeans against the panty-wrapped sweetness she teased him with. The crowd went wild as the song reached a crescendo, soon drowned out by the cheering.

Louise was so aroused and couldn't resist, seizing the opportunity presented by the lull before the next song began.

"Follow me?" she said, posing it as a question and assuming he would refuse.

He nodded.

As the crowd surged they fought their way through it. Louise never letting go of the stranger's hand, weaving through the ocean of sweating bodies until they burst into an anonymous breeze-block corridor and the delicious cool air beyond. There were plenty of gig-goers out here, catching a breath or heading to and from the bar and bathroom facilities.

Louise led them up the corridor and pulled a sharp right into one of the male toilets, far enough away from the main points of entry to the hall as to be currently empty. Within a heartbeat she had locked the cubicle door behind them and forced him down onto the seat; she giggled when she saw that his jeans had darkened with moisture where she had been rubbing against the knot of his erection, now looking like it was ready to tear through the denim in order to reach her.

"Send me the dry cleaning bill," she teased, quickly unfastening his jeans and letting his cock spill out, eight fat inches of white meat as hard as diamond. With no warning she gripped it and sank it into her throat and he bucked, clutching the porcelain beneath him to steady himself and trying not to scream in delight.

She sucked him three or four times to lube him up with saliva, her lip stain smearing him with cherry-red streaks. That was all she needed; this would be fast, hard, quick and beyond belief for both of them. She held his shoulder to steady herself as she tugged the gusset of her panties aside and sank swiftly onto him, glimmering lips parting to accommodate.

"Fucking hell," he seethed in her ear. She had to bite into his shoulder to keep from crying out as his colossal cock rose up into her. Listening to the muffled rhythm of the music echoing through the building she set herself into a synchronous pattern, hips grinding in unison. He rolled her skirt higher so he could grip her plush cheeks, fingers squeezing so hard she yelped in exquisite pain. Her tight tunnel was reamed each time his steely penetrating tool slid within. Her huge tits, stretched within the T-shirt, rolled against his muscular chest and he allowed his face to sink into the hidden cleavage as she rode him.

Then he gripped her by the hair and tugged her head back so he could see her. His eyes were intense and she held him in thrall with her own, watching each other and enjoying every rising sensation. Every nerve in both their bodies felt like it was on fire, and she could feel her pulse in her sopping nethers, shifting her speed to ride the sensation so each downward grind matched her heartbeat.

The band reached the song's crescendo at the same time as they did, and the stranger's rocket launched inside her, shooting a hot volume of beautiful spunk into the orbit of her body. Her silken purse sealed tight around him to steal every drop, and the crowd roared its delight at their mutual, intense climax.

Their sweating foreheads pressed together and she kissed him deeply, loving the feeling of those bristles round his mouth barbing her chin. When finally they broke their clinch he was able to introduce himself.

"I'm Joseph," he said, panting.

"Louise."

He laughed quietly. "Louise, I know now's probably not the best time to tell you, but I'm married."

"I know," she said, lifting his left hand from her ass and waving it in front of his face. His wedding ring glinted in the strip lighting of the arena bathroom. "I don't care if you don't."

*

Louise could barely breathe, her pussy white-hot with sensation at remembering what had happened in that cramped cubicle. She was certain she could feel, against the flesh of her belly, the wetness of Sophie's aroused quim through the rip in her tights. This was turning the dominant woman on in no short order.

"Kiss her," Sophie demanded breathily, swept away in the recollections as much as Louise was. "Kiss her like you don't kiss me."

Joseph obeyed his wife, plunging his tongue against Louise's, brawling within the enclaves of their mouth. He reached under her pendulous breasts and tweaked at her nipples in the way that always worked wonders for her. She groaned into his mouth.

Sophie cast the book to the floor with a heavy thud and her hands came back with a purpose, one of them spreading the cheeks of Louise's dense ass, the other homing in on the folds of her aching box. For the first time ever, Sophie delved into a honey pot that was not her own, somewhat directly but with no small amount of pleasure. Louise's vocal delight was uncontainable, roaring her glee as Joseph held her hair tightly and continued his kiss.

"You want his cock, don't you?" Sophie teased, elbow working feverishly, her arm thrusting. Louise could only grunt incoherently as two of Sophie's fingers slid in and out of her with audible, sloppy sounds; they were flat to the lower wall of her, curving down as if trying to reach her bellybutton, easily finding the spongy mound of her g-spot, at the very same time that the pad of Sophie's thumb found her exposed and quivering clit.

Louise came with the intensity of a hundred thunderstorms,

lighting sparking her vision as relentless vibrations spread from the tight canal of her pussy, reaching out to every nerve ending. She became aware of the sound she was making, low at first building to a high, open-mouthed howl. Control was gone, lost in the tumult of sensations so powerful she desired to live in this moment from now until the end of time. In the psychological centres of her brain still capable of thought amongst the firing synapses and flooding endorphins, she thought: *I've never come like that before...*

As a sense of control returned in tiny increments, she realised she was being led now, hips guided by Joseph's firm hands and led by Sophie with a handful of her hair. The wife lay down, head supported on her plush pillows, in the centre of the bed, spreading her legs wide, showing off her flexibility. She clutched at her own tights and ripped them across her thighs in several places to complete the effect of a woman ravaged by her new encounters, and widened the gash around her pussy, a garden beaded with her natural dew.

"Go down on me," she said, hand unyielding atop Louise's head. "Make me come again while my husband fills you up."

At his wife's behest Joe climbed onto the bed behind Louise, who raised her hips to his approach. All three of them were naked now but for Louise's seamed holdups and Sophie's bra and ripped tights. They were three carriages of a train about to dock.

Joe's engorged rod plunged into the searing pool of Louise's twitching, tightening pussy, all the way up to his pelvis. The resulting cry was stifled as Sophie pulled her mouth onto her moisture-dappled well, and the vibrations made by the choked sound made Sophie squeal in ecstatic joy. Louise looked at Sophie over the gradual slope of her body and the mounds of her small breasts; the wife released her tits from the bra and tweaked her own nipples fiercely as the mistress' tongue slithered within her. She looked enraptured in what was taking place in a bedroom usually devoid of anything even remotely as rampant as this. She would hold Louise's gaze a while then shift to her husband, pumping away at the entrance of this other woman with rhythmic, urgent thrusts of his hips. Louise was a conduit between them, channeling something long unspoken, seething and desperate to be brought to light, the instrument of their sexual salvation. The whole notion of being their aid, their toy, drove her wild beyond compare and she couldn't hold back her words.

"Fuck my cunt," she cried, breaking from Sophie's twinkling

ribbon of pink delight. She knew many women who balked at the word but she was all for reclaiming it, loving how dirty it sounded, how raw and slutty it made her feel to say it. The others were similarly roused by it. "Use me, both of you."

Sophie held the mistress in place to allow her expert ministrations to bring her closer to a creaming climax, each flick of her tongue causing her to gasp and squeal. Joseph took a firmer, copious handful of her pliant hips and thrust harder while the air in the room took on take on a static, electrical energy, as three natural conductors primed themselves for discharge. Louise's whole world was spinning as her body ratcheted towards orgasm once more, and she sensed the synchronicity between their trio.

It was simultaneous and all-encompassing, three voices ululating with intense pleasure. Louise's cunt squeezed in pulsating waves around Joseph's cock as it cannoned its fluid shots against her contracting walls. She felt Sophie's velvet folds twitch as her own spark ignited; she gushed a tiny fount of translucent fem-cum across Louise's chin and victorious tongue and squealed a strident, joyful note.

Three chests heaved in unison, three minds wandered the heady realm of post-orgasmic bliss on their own, incapable for this wonderful, numb interlude of anything resembling rational thought.

Louise's orgasm subsided just in time to feel herself rolled aside by husband and wife. It was not an aggressive gesture. They were simply clearing the space between them, ready now to close the distance, unable to control being swept towards each other. The gap closed. Louise rolled onto her back as Joe fell upon his wife, their lips meeting hungrily, twin sheens of sweat becoming one fine film between bodies that had not made this kind of contact in so long. Her thighs clamped him, calves locking behind his ass, pulling him closer, and Louise watched Joe's cock, slick with her own resin and traces of his cum, sink into Sophie's spasming furrow, unable to wither in the face of such arousal. They roiled against one another, arching their backs, interlocking, unified.

Louise chose to leave them to it, to rediscover what they had lost. With the couple oblivious to her motions, she slid on her skirt, feeling Joseph's sweat drying on her thighs, his seed trickling from her secret lips, and knowing it was the last time she would ever have a part of him within her. She did not feel hurt in any way, or even disappointed, but somehow wholly satisfied.

She slid on her corset and tightened it quickly, then left the lovers alone, padding down the stairs. With a smile at the sound of creaking bedsprings, a headboard thumping against the bedroom wall, and the married couple's rising cries, she made sure she did not forget her coat on the way out.

PAINTED
A Poem

Coated with stain,
That forever remains
On my soul each time,
I make those lips mine.

You entice, and draw in
And then we begin,
As I taste, with a quiver,
Breath escaping that sliver

Of a perfect, sweet smile
That soothes and soon riles
Every sense that I own.
And elicits such moans.

I brush those fine lips.
My tongue darts and dips,
It probes and it tastes
And it will never waste

A drop of your soul,
As it makes us one, whole,
Complete, bound yet free,
Together…you…me…

Leave on me your brand,
I make this demand.
Target, don't miss me.
Now dammit, girl…kiss me.

ABOUT THE AUTHOR

Cameron Lincoln is a gentleman writer in a variety of genres including romantic erotica.

He recently released a poetry anthology entitled MINE: BODY & SOUL, which became a #1 Amazon bestseller on its first day.

He is currently working on his first full length novel, set in the paranormal romance/urban fantasy genre, entitled THE MAYFLY.

He lives in England.

Find his official website at www.cameron-lincoln.com

Follow him on Twitter @Cameron_Lincoln and on Facebook at facebook.com/cameronlincolnwriter

Printed in Great Britain
by Amazon.co.uk, Ltd.,
Marston Gate.